# Corrosive Minds

## Vonnie Giles

U P Publications
2020

This book is dedicated to my beloved parents,

thanking them for all the love and care they gave

me and the sacrifices they made for me

# Corrosive Minds

A selection of Macabre and Visceral Horror Stories by Vonnie Giles.

Following Vonnie's successful short story compilations *Acid Rain* and *Tightly Bound* and her contributions to the anthology *Picked and Mixed*, Vonnie has collected together another selection of her unique short stories. This is Vonnie at her darkest and most corrosive – so the content is definitely adult... Caveat Emptor – you have been warned!

Corrosive Minds delves into her eclectic collection of dark and esoteric tales and promises to horrify.

Meet some of the darkest characters ever to send shivers into your nightmares.

Author of Acid Rain and Tightly Bound

See all Vonnie's books on
www.uppbooks.com
www.vonniegiles.com

All Rights Reserved

No part of this publication may be reproduced or transmitted by any means, electronic, mechanical, photocopy or otherwise, without the prior permission of the publisher. This is a work of fiction. Names, characters, places and incidents other than historical are either the product of the author's imagination or are used fictitiously. Any resemblance to actual persons, living or dead, business establishments, events, or locales is entirely coincidental.

First published in Great Britain in 2020 by U P Publications
St George's House, George Street, Huntingdon, Cambs. PE29 3GH

Cover design copyright © G Griffin Peers

Copyright © Shirley (Vonnie) Giles 2019, 2020

Shirley (Vonnie) Giles has asserted her moral rights

A CIP Catalogue record of this book is available from the
British Library
ISBN 978-1-912777-45-7

Also published as an ebook by U P Publications under
ISBN 978-1-912777-46-4

FIRST PAPERBACK EDITION
Published by U P Publications
www.uppbooks.com
www.vonniegiles.com

# Contents

A Shining Death ............................................................ 7
A Village Tale ............................................................... 17
A Wet Weekend in Hell ............................................... 25
Altar of Memory ........................................................... 34
Blind Date ..................................................................... 39
Bocanegra ..................................................................... 49
Conrad's War ................................................................ 56
Exposure Time .............................................................. 68
Fertility .......................................................................... 77
Grey World .................................................................... 83
Henry ............................................................................. 90
Her Name was Aphrodite ............................................ 96
Inamorata ...................................................................... 104
Strange Trick of Light .................................................. 117
The Changing Sea ........................................................ 127
The Enemy .................................................................... 136
The Lord of Death ........................................................ 144
**The Mausoleum** ............................................................ 152
The Unfortunate Wife .................................................. 159
When He Sleeps ........................................................... 167
Who Said That? ............................................................ 175

# A Shining Death

Hearing someone approaching behind her she looked back at me, elegant and smiling, but I was afraid of her no longer. She had been my model and my muse; indeed, once the obsession that I felt for her was so strong that it had frightened me. Her power over me, however, had gradually faded away with time, for I had not seen her for months. I still loved her, of course, but not quite with the same passion.

They say that absence makes the heart grow fonder, but obviously not in my case. Life has to go on and I am always resilient in my disappointments. However, I am by nature obsessively jealous and full of envy and so it did me no good at all that sitting opposite her, naturally at the same luncheon table, was her latest lover. He was no doubt some rich patron of the arts to judge from the fine cut and expensive cloth of his suit. His greying beard told the world that he favoured younger women, (well, don't most men?) especially one as lovely as Martine with her rosebud mouth and dark, shining hair swept up: her crowning glory topped by a red-feathered hat that matched the red feathery corsage worn on her dress.

She was surprised and, apparently by the look on her face, pleased to see me . . . *but it is too late, my darling, for you should have accepted the offer while it was there! Turn your beautiful head to the right and you will see my new love, her glass of wine held elegantly in her soft hand.*

The restaurant terrace was seething with patrons for it was the great day when we artists finally had seen our paintings hanging in the prestigious gallery. The tradition was to add the finishing touches to them there and then, varnishing them, if we so wished, as a protection from dust, dirt and age. My painting was of Martine, her elbow resting on her knee while she stared deep into my eyes. Now she was framed and varnished for the world to see. In the gallery what a buzz of excitement had filled the air as our friends, our rich sponsors and our even richer potential buyers witnessed this final phase, like some theatrical preview!

Now came the celebratory luncheon that marked the end of our efforts before the exhibition was formerly opened to the public the next day. Le Doyen was the most prestigious restaurant in Paris, with large neo-classical statues adorning its entrance and raised banks of pink and white flowers decorating the terrace.

All that remained was for us to enjoy the end of our labours, artistically speaking. Gentlemen in top hats milled around the beautiful open space, cigar smoke filling the air and vying with the expensive fragrance of the ladies. Here and there were glimpsed the fine, polished helmets of military men. The waiters, meanwhile, in their long, white aprons, were busily uncorking bottles of wine and carrying in small dishes of delicacies such as truffles, foie gras and escargots that were to begin the luncheon. People were arriving in droves and some no doubt would be forced to lunch inside the restaurant itself – but, beautiful as it was, the best tables were on the terrace. That was where the highest of high society and the cultural élite of Paris discussed the paintings that they had viewed, arguing over the merits and faults of each one. Even Monsieur Rodin, the noted sculptor, was heard giving his opinions.

I stood behind Martine and picked up her hand that was resting on the tablecloth. I lifted it to my lips to kiss it and again could feel the familiar emotions of sexual desire and also, unexpectedly, the terrible regret that she was no longer mine.

My new love, seated at the table next to us where I would at any moment join her, watched me and knew immediately what I was feeling. She turned her eyes upon Martine's escort; looking him up and down, wondering what advantage he had over me. Was it worthwhile, she was wondering, to try and elbow her way into his affections? He was rich (no doubt of that) distinguished and, in his ageing way, quite attractive.

As the luncheon progressed and the noise of talking increased around us, our lips were loosened by the wine and liqueurs. Before long the four of us were engaged in easy conversation and two waiters were not happy when asked to move our tables together.

I had taken an instant dislike to Martine's friend, Monsieur Aubert, with his apparent distant connection to some noble family of which I had never heard, but he ate his food like a peasant so I did wonder about his pedigree.

Looking closely at Martine, I was beginning to think that I was not at all well and had this sudden fear for my sanity. The most horrendous idea, the most satanic image had been placed in my mind. Nevertheless, I was incredibly excited by the prospect of what I was going to do – and make no mistake; I would do it, come what may!

This delightful occasion had now soured and all the joy had left my soul. I would, however, find satisfaction, both artistically and psychologically, in what I had decided to do. I must allow my new love to exercise her charms upon Monsieur Aubert, for I no longer needed her; he was obviously a far better choice for her than this humble, though successful, artist.

As evening approached the long luncheon came to an end. My new love had made her choice and she and Monsieur Aubert left together, perhaps to go to the Paris Opera, perhaps not, allowing Martine and me to renew our former relationship, but I knew this would not happen. Martine stood swinging her handbag carelessly by her side in a gesture of carefree happiness, giving me an enticing, come-hither look. *You needn't bother, my dear, it's too late for that – the die has been cast.*

I had been fortunate to find rich, loyal patrons who swore that I was one of the best painters alive whose talent would enhance their considerable fortunes and make mine. Hence my lovely house, its glowing carriage lamps and hanging baskets of flowers making it dream-like on that glorious summer evening.

Down the wooden stairs of my spacious studio we went. I sat Martine down upon the white sofa. She studied the gilt-framed paintings that decorated the room, some still stacked randomly against the walls. She saw her own image in most of them, but one or two were landscapes that had been especially commissioned. An upright piano stood in a corner with a vase of sunflowers and lavender on top.

The smell of oil paint and turpentine-soaked rags filled the air, and Martine looked at the easels, dirty brushes and stretched canvases as though she had never seen them before. During my happiest of times, however, this atelier had been almost her second home.

We clinked our glasses of absinthe together as a toast to the end of a memorable day, though not as memorable as it would become when the news hit the headlines, but poor Martine wouldn't know anything about that.

A great deal of work still remained to be done, so it would be a long, emotional night. The moon shone through the huge window that was wonderfully situated to draw in the light, which is a given for any artist.

Martine was ready to receive my advances, fired up by all the wine and liqueurs she had consumed during the day, but she had betrayed me, rejected me, and for what? For a pretentious parvenu, as remote from a noble family as I was!

I put one of my hands around the back of her neck as she leaned forward expecting a kiss. I whispered to her, "You shouldn't have done it, Martine, you really shouldn't." Her eyes widened with pleasure, as I placed my other hand on the front of her smooth throat. She smiled as I clasped her neck tightly thinking it was the beginning of a little game that we always loved to play, but now it would far surpass her expectations. I squeezed and squeezed as hard as I could, but it was too late for her to struggle, for I twisted and twisted until her eyes looked as though they would pop out of their sockets. "I know we all have to die sometime, Martine, and I'm truly sorry about this. But by tomorrow you and I will be immortal, never to be forgotten. A unique work of art will have been created – you as the centre piece, I as the originator." She lost consciousness and with a final wrench I broke her neck.

Out of breath with my exertions I undressed her, humming a little tune to myself. I then put on my smock and went to collect the tins of varnish I kept in a cupboard under the stairs. Carefully and lovingly, I thickly covered the front of her body with the varnish. It would take hours to dry properly and, even then, would probably feel tacky, but I needed my creation for the public opening of the exhibition tomorrow, so decided not to bother varnishing the back of her body.

The moon shone through the great window onto the shining corpse, varnished as I like all my works to be, but this was my greatest creation. To pass the time, I sat at the piano and played some of Chopin's études, not very well, as I'm not much of a musician, but it helped the time to pass. A few hours later, as dawn began to appear in the sky, I knew I had no time to spare and must make haste.

I knocked on the door in the basement where the poor idiot who did my odd jobs was living. We covered the body with a beautiful, red, velvet curtain and with some difficulty placed it in the back of a carriage. My fingers felt sticky which greatly upset me, but I still knew that the work would be perfection personified.

The next morning the public crowded into the exhibition and most important of all came the prospective buyers. Which of them would buy the varnished body of Martine that I and my idiot helper had placed on the gallery wall? Who would take her home, forever to admire her beauty and to wonder at my genius? Someone had just at that very moment removed the velvet curtain, so that suddenly there she was revealed for all to see with the sun shining on her nakedness. She was like Eve in paradise for a tall potted palm stood next to her helping to evoke an image of the Garden of Eden. The only problem was that her neck looked rather strange and that some of the varnish had trickled down, making a little pool in her navel. I looked at her from behind the dumbstruck observers and murmured loving words under my breath. *My muse, my model, my inspiration, my love, my betrayer, this is where you truly belong.*

Then, feeling rather dazed, I stepped forward, faced my admirers and spoke feelingly the words that had come into my mind.

*Her body white and lustrous,*
*How death upon her shines,*
*Immortal flesh that will never whither,*
*So she will hang thus here forever.*

Reality then came like a bolt from the blue; I was suddenly aware of hissing and booing and screaming coming from the crowd, for now they understood what they were actually seeing. I was really afraid, for undoubtedly the gendarmerie would soon be on my tail – then what would happen: perpetual imprisonment or the guillotine, for one did not escape what I had done without some sort of punishment? I could see that now.

At this very moment in time I am awaiting a priest to give me absolution for my heinous crime, before my head is separated from my body by that arch-bitch Madame Guillotine. I have decided, in fact, that all women are bitches sent here by the devil to tempt us. Whatever is to come in the afterlife cannot, however, be much worse than the crowded, squalid, rat-infested cell where I have been living my last days. I am thus trying to keep a stiff upper lip as the English would express it, but it's no good saying I'm not afraid, because I am – frightened to death, in fact.

# A Village Tale

Dinosaurs didn't make noises… So, you see, there was no growling, no grunting, no terrifying roaring. Indeed, the home of these huge creatures was probably a fairly silent place. Everyone said Doctor Slurry was mad to expect a Nobel Prize for his revelation of this fact, but then he is mad, completely off his rocker. Hence his permanent sojourn in this sad place where his family has placed him.

You must have guessed where he is, from the awful screaming and the constant moaning that you can probably hear in the background. When all the windows are open it permeates the valleys, unsettling the cattle and the birds, disturbing the well-to-do landowners in their big houses and the villagers in their more humble dwellings.

Did you know that the dinosaurs had coloured skin, not the boring browns and greys that you usually see in pictures? Mainly they were striped red and white, or so the experts say. Doctor Slurry's scientific knowledge, however, tells him that they were psychedelic, in fact, not too different from this place. When he wakes in the mornings everything is normal but, after his breakfast medication, all the colours of an amazingly vivid and varied rainbow appear. A sure message from the past that he's got it all correct!

Today is his Auntie Hermione's day for visiting. She comes once a week, shambling along in her drab clothes. He's rather ashamed of her and wishes she wouldn't come. If only she'd take a leaf out of the dinosaurs' book and brighten herself up a bit. She also is an expert on the prehistoric age, but like him the light in her brain is slowly dimming. There's no doubt that soon she will be occupying one of these rather pleasant rooms.

She is sitting in his favourite chair which annoyed him no end, so that things weren't off to a good start. As she jabbered away about nothing, his attention totally switched off …he was much more interested in watching a bluebottle buzzing away on the window. If he killed it, a nasty, squashy, yellow mess would be left on the glass.

He thought it was a pity there were no carnivorous plants decorating his room; he was fascinated by those meat-eating wonders! They would tackle anything to keep starvation at bay:

insects, snakes, small, furry mammals. You name it, they'd eat it!

When Doctor Slurry looked again at the window there was a second bluebottle crawling over its surface. Too lethargic to swat it, he merely flicked a newspaper in its direction and both flies took flight. The room was hot and airless and gradually a strange, sweet, intoxicating scent that he couldn't identify assailed his nostrils.

He glanced over at Auntie, for she was never what one might describe as fragrant, usually giving off a stale, sweaty smell. He was surprised that she would bother buying such fragrant niceties. She had definitely been getting up to something for her right hand was sparkling in the sunlight that shone into the room. Wasting her pension on cheap fripperies and bling, he supposed. Surely at this late stage she wasn't trying to attract a man.

He looked around for his glasses so he could see better just what she'd been buying. His shaking hands fumbled in the large, droopy pockets of his psychedelic cardigan, full of old tissues, coins, cigarette butts and newspaper cuttings and there, at the bottom covered in ash, were his half-glasses.

Even so, he couldn't quite make out what he

was looking at. It seemed as if the flesh on Auntie's right hand was sprouting and he could see feathery tentacles with blobs of what looked like sparkling sequins on the end of each one.

The bluebottles' buzzing increased in volume and they sang loudly in unison, until one of them suddenly went too near one of the blobs. It became well and truly stuck, despite its desperate struggle to escape from the gluey prison. The second bluebottle followed suit, and there was Auntie's hand with two flies performing a sticky dance of death on its surface.

Doctor Slurry was so fascinated that he struggled to his feet to take a closer at what he was seeing. The hand itself looked extremely unhealthy, rather like a portion of green, mushy peas. Feathery tentacles and glittering blobs were by this time increasing at a great speed and completely enclosing the bluebottles. Not a pleasant way to die thought Doctor Slurry, but then we've all got to go sometime!

Auntie Hermione was looking distinctly under the weather, gazing uncomprehendingly at her hand which, now too heavy for her arm, had drooped towards the floor. At least, it had shut her up and there was a blissful silence.

Raptors were, relatively speaking, small dinosaurs, not giants like Tyrannosaurus Rex, which is just as well, otherwise Doctor Slurry would never have been able to leave his room again. He had looked away from Auntie Hermione's gruesome hand, only to gaze in wonder at his own body, at his now torn clothes through which he could clearly see his own skin. It was leathery and had turned a very peculiar shade of navy-blue decorated with thin, wavy red and white stripes.

He wanted to sit down to recover from the shock, but a splendid tail prevented this, so there he had to stand on his two hind legs with small, clawed forearms held out in front of him. Suddenly and disappointedly, he gave a loud roar, proving that his hope of winning the Nobel Prize was forever doomed. The noise was so resounding that it bounced across to the opposite hills and back again.

The commotion this caused in the home and around the village can only be imagined. The matron, a good sensible woman, thought she must be hallucinating and the staff went into total turmoil, all of them expecting to wake up at any moment in their beds to find that it had been a very vivid nightmare.

The local paper had a field day and, for the first time ever, had an exclusive story that would rock the world. Jim, who reported on everything from births, marriages and deaths to the occasional break-in, had definite visions of being called to London to further his career in the competitive world of the mass media.

However, there was a village informer out to make a bit of money and so, within an hour or two, all the major news broadcasters and the Daily Balderdash Online were at Jim's heels. Even these hardened delvers into people's lives were shocked by what they saw. They hung from the roof and erected ladders and platforms to get the best possible footage. This was undoubtedly the highlight of their careers, even better than the suspected visitations from aliens, for they were on sure, solid ground with this story.

In fact, there had never been a story like it before, and the world was absolutely fascinated, people coming in droves to see what they could see. Cars, coaches, hikers; they all came along and fortunately spent so much money in the village that there was soon an epidemic of new clothes, cars and even houses among the villagers. Everyone seemed to benefit from the event; it was almost better than winning the lottery.

Why all this should have happened to this perfectly harmless pair is a complete mystery.

They have been prodded and probed by virtually every scientist in the country, some of whom have even questioned them verbally which, as you can imagine, was a pretty fruitless exercise.

Poor Auntie Hermione's brain had given up the struggle to think thoughts and Doctor Slurry's raptor tongue made trying to speak just not worth the bother. A solution, it would seem, is still a long way off.

In the meantime, they have now returned to the home where, after the initial shock, everyone has become quite used to them. Every day you can see Doctor Slurry pushing Auntie Hermione's wheelchair around the village. As the weight of her hand pulls her downwards and to one side, it is completely impossible for her to walk properly. Much easier for the hand to rest on her lap and for her to be wheeled through the streets; as long as Doctor Slurry is careful not dig her in the back with his sharp claws.

They have even found a source of employment. Any villager whose house has an infestation, be it mice, ants or whatever, always sends for Auntie Hermione whose irresistibly-scented hand immediately brings a solution that cannot be denied. Not only this, but on many a day Doctor Slurry can be seen in the middle of a field, waving his tail around and giving the occasional decibel-defying roar – much better than any scarecrow.

Thus, the odd couple lead a strange but useful life and are really quite happy with their lot. Anyway, they are both too batty to know the difference.

# A Wet Weekend in Hell

The moon shone down upon the beach wondering about all the noise and commotion that was filling the usually tranquil scene that lay beneath it. The lighthouse, too, cast brilliance onto the water, its flashing, rotating signal giving out a warning of danger to those on the sea. However, tonight the danger was of a different order and the damage had already been done, for both the lighthouse and the moon were illuminating a woman's body. She was surrounded by police officers whose cars gave out their own visual warning that anyone sensible should keep out of the way.

Mrs Lytten-Berry would never again live in her cloud-cuckoo-land and would never again look with pride upon her husband wearing his mayoral chain. Her bruised body had been washed up onto to the beach and left for some poor, late-night dog walker to discover.

Looking down upon the whole scene from the

coastal hills were the weekenders' cottages. They lined the picturesque, crooked streets that were so loved by the well-heeled visitors from the big city. It was beginning to rain again as it had been doing for most of the weekend, but the sea, as yet, was untouched by waves.

Mrs Lytten-Berry, before her unfortunate demise, had spent most of the afternoon pressing and pushing her not inconsiderable frame against that of her husband. She had thought of herself as an attractive sexual creature. Unknown to her, however, the mayor had, rather unsuccessfully, been trying to fantasise that she was Maureen, who was not only his mistress, but also the Borough Surveyor. Now, what a wife she would have been; a true trophy wife, in fact almost as good looking as Mrs Trump!

Somewhere nearby, behind a rock, Maureen sat in her stylishly patterned wetsuit watching all the comings and goings on the beach. Well, that was a job well done, she thought. Old Mrs L-B gone off to the great knackers' yard in the sky! Nevertheless, she had been surprised at her victim's quick return from the water, for she had always understood that it took days or even weeks for a body to reappear.

Meanwhile, Jay-Jay, as the Mayor was known, having heard the news after a visit from the police, sat in the council office crying his eyes out; not from sorrow for his loss, because she was no loss, but for his guilt because he'd not played fair. He should have accepted her, warts and all. She had worked very hard to support him and had never once let him down, whereas he had for some years been rather ashamed of her and had been carrying on disgracefully He was, however, a man with a man's needs and just doing what all men did. At one time she must have been definite arm candy; otherwise he would never have married her.

She had still thought of herself as the cat's whiskers. She was the mayor's wife and therefore almost on a par with royalty, but unknown to her she had simply become mutton dressed up as lamb: lamb that was long, long out of date.

The dead body lying on the beach was still bearing witness to this, although the twin set with pearls and the perm and also the corsets that in her mind brought perfection to her plump shape, had now lost their pristine state; Maureen had seen to that. The mayoress knew that Jay-Jay had his little interests outside the home and the council office, but she never asked him about it – probably did not want to know.

Jay-jay decided that he would spend what was left of the night curled up in the mayoral chair, dressed up in his robe and tricorn hat, as a sort of tribute to her, because she had been so proud of his position which made her lowly start in a council house seem a whole world away. In front of him was a half empty bottle of fine whisky. Or should that be a half full bottle of fine whisky, because he was now free to follow his wicked way with Maureen or, indeed, with any other woman who took his fancy? He could undoubtedly now look forward to a life of hedonism, untinged with guilt.

Maureen waded from her hiding place and after a couple of quick strokes had swum onto the beach. The police and the body had now disappeared, and she was free to wander across the sand, glorying in the thought that Jay-Jay was finally hers. She had never really discovered why the mayor's consort liked to go shell-collecting every Saturday afternoon at about six o' clock except, of course, for those times, when there was some official weekend event when she would do her duty and accompany Jay-Jay on his mission. She had been a creature of habit and it had thus been easy to locate her, to grab her and to drag her into the sea – the silly cow had never learned how to swim, so she'd had no one to blame but herself.

A light sprinkling of rain continued to fall from the sky and a wind began to blow, causing waves to ride upon the water. Maureen loved anything to do with the sea and filled with happiness, the murderess began to sing to herself.

Suddenly, an unbelievably vile smell accosted her and she felt a hand on her shoulder that made her start in surprise. She almost fainted at the sight of Mrs L-B. This was an impossibility for she had been collected and removed by an ambulance! Why, she had only been in the water for a few hours and logically should not, of course, have surfaced so soon and scientifically should not have decomposed so unbelievably quickly.

Her already putrefying body was green and swollen, covered in blisters and her lips and eyes were covered with crabs and small fish were feasting joyfully on her flesh.

"Well, Maureen, that wasn't a nice thing to do, was it! A fine Borough Surveyor you've turned out to be. I'd have thought that someone with your intelligence would not have resorted to murder. Here you are with geometry, trigonometry, law, physics and heaven know what else at your fingertips and all for nothing. Because you must realise, of course, that everyone knows of your shenanigans with Jay-Jay and that you will spend the rest of your life in prison. You could, of course, just walk into the water and join me for eternity, until he comes to meet us in the great hereafter!"

"Get away from me!" shouted Maureen as the remains of her last meal suddenly appeared on the sand and she continued to retch and heave at the sight and smell of the revolting apparition.

The next time she looked up, the devilish figure had disappeared into thin air and the only smell was that of the sea.

She was either going mad, dreaming or going to be haunted for the rest of her life by this fiendish ghost – and she did not even believe in ghosts – at least not until now! Meanwhile at that very same moment the coroner, having been dragged from his bed at this unearthly hour, was examining the authentic body of the town's leading lady. This definitely looked as though it could be a case of murder. Like everyone else he was privy to Jay-Jay's goings-on with the Borough Surveyor and actually envied him, for she was a very juicy, foxy little woman. Most people in the town had at one time or another seen her in various snazzy wetsuits on the beach. She immediately became the police's prime suspect, for she had the most to gain.

Unless it had been Jay-Jay himself; with murder you could never rule out anything. Hopefully, the forensic evidence would soon make everything clear.

Maureen, now changed into one of her favourite outfits, made the fine mayoral home her first port of call, but the house was empty, so although it was only half past seven on that rainy Sunday morning, she headed for the council offices. Only the caretaker wanting to earn overtime pay was there, sweeping the entrance with a broom. He said that he had not set eyes on the mayor, but she thought he was probably in the mayor's rather grand chamber – which indeed he was. They were going to be the last sane moments that Maureen would ever experience.

The fine oak walls with their paintings of past mayors were covered in a strange, greenish slime and most of the chairs on which the councillors sat for official meetings were overturned.

Then, unfortunately for her, Maureen turned her eyes up to the dais where the mayor's chair stood. What she saw was Jay-Jay dressed in his splendid fur-edged, red robe squashed against the back wall. His arms were spread out as though he had been crucified, and pressing him against the wall was a huge octopus with sharp, pointed yellow teeth. It was something you would only see in a horror film.

Her screams must have reached across to the lovely cottages and down to the sea to be heard by whatever was lingering in the water. This however, was no film, but real life and those who were later to view the body would never quite recover from the scene.

The caretaker never recovered at all, for he suffered a serious stroke and lost the ability to speak again or, indeed, to walk again. Later, on that Sunday morning, they all watched as the octopus gradually disappeared into thin air as though it had never existed. It was like a magician's trick. The body it left behind was not a pretty sight.

The Borough Surveyor was later found guilty of Mrs Lytten-Berry's murder. There had been no court appearance for she had been deemed too mentally impaired to stand trial and was sectioned to a mental institution for the rest of her life.

Hell is a burning furnace and not something usually associated with rain, but that wet weekend in Jay-Jay's beloved little town proved that there are exceptions to every rule. Each night, thereafter, the moon continued to help the light house send forth a radiance onto the beach, but for a long time it would wonder at the strange scenes it had witnessed. It had seen plenty of bodies washed ashore, but the incredibly strange, slimy octopus that had flipped and flopped its way through the empty streets as dawn broke had been in a class of its own.

# Altar of Memory

On the skeleton of a leafless dried-up tree, a pair of owls resting hooted into the darkness. The acrid smell of smoke filled the air, the garbage gently burning. Foxes, starving dogs, vermin – nature's scavengers of the night – they were all there, gathered at the refuse tip, chancing their luck, searching for their fair share of what was on offer as the hump-backed, gibbous moon looked down upon them. What was unacceptable for them would, during daylight hours, find an easy market among the down-and-outs of the city who would take anything that they could use or barter.

Meanwhile, living in an utterly different world, not fifty miles away, was Francis – soft music playing in his smart apartment that overlooked the tree-lined river. It was midnight for him, just as it was for the little hunters among the refuse.

"I love you, Jeannie," he whispered…as the rats and the weasels that lived nearby went about their nightly tasks. "I always will – through all eternity!" He stood facing her, slightly to one side, his right arm around her waist and the other at his side. His lips were turned down as if he were at any moment going to weep. Jeannie, his love, his life, was dressed in the beautiful, blue gown that he most liked to see her wear and, hanging around her throat, the diamond necklace he had given to her the day he realised he couldn't live without her. At the side of them was a small table on which stood just one single glass of bubbling champagne and an ash tray with just one single cigarette smouldering away.

"Shall we dance, sweetheart? It's 'Jealousy' – your favourite." He nuzzled her neck with his face, kissing her breasts, his hips beginning to move in time to the music.

Francis, a man of so many talents and so many secrets to whom discretion was a way of life! Never try to deceive him because the tone of your voice would have given you away, never try to smooth-talk him because he was the world's greatest cynic. He could study your body language and read your face as expertly as any first-class poker player, know all about you from a single glance. All in all, attributes that were indispensable in the murky world of espionage to which he belonged. He, therefore, knew that

Jeannie was as honest and true as the day was long. There would never be anyone as adorable as she was.

So, there he was in the dimly lit room, his head now on her shoulder, his arms clasped tightly, desperately, around her, his feet tapping more and more urgently on the parquet floor as the tempo of the tango increased.

Then, all at once, the barking of a distant fox could be heard through the open sliding-doors as his tears started to fall and the sobbing began. His hands moved over the silky material of her gown, over her headless, armless, legless body, over the metal armature that was the tailor's dummy which every day was dressed in a different outfit. In a few moments it would be her wedding dress that would adorn it, commemorating the day just a year ago when her life had ended; shot on the steps of the church by one of the bad guys, the blood stains still visible on the white lace. Obviously, not such a discreet spy as he'd believed himself to be – his undercover activities less than fool proof!

The haunting notes of the music faded away and Francis sat down, contemplating the shadows in front of him and the emptiness within him. He exchanged the sparkle of the champagne for the sharp sourness of bourbon and gave himself up fully to his misery. Life was a void, a nothingness without her. He did not even have the will or the energy for revenge; what would be the point? An empty victory that would never bring her back!

A solitary owl had alighted on the railing of the balcony outside and was gazing into the room, its presence unheeded, while Francis, standing up again, slipped the blue gown from the rigid, lifeless body, letting it lie in an untidy heap at his feet. Then he replaced it with her beautiful wedding gown. How wondrous she had looked in it; until the moment when fate had cruelly destroyed his happiness. He let his fingers wander lovingly over the metal lattice work, willing his imagination to let him feel her soft body, but it was a fruitless effort for, only at night, in the world of dreams was he ever able to touch her smooth skin, to smell the gorgeous scent of Shalimar, to feel her sweet breath on his face…

…Two short months later, on a chilly, fog-laden October morning, a carrion crow, hovering over the smouldering detritus of the refuse tip, spied something of interest among the filth and began to peck at a grubby, bloodstained wedding dress. It was not worth the effort, however, and it was soon left to rot, together with the torn, blue dress that lay crumpled beneath it.

On the other hand, Sam, itinerant vagrant, long-time human scavenger, had much more luck than the crow and was really quite delighted with the tailor's dummy that he had just glimpsed under a pile of old matting. It was beginning to go rusty, but with a little tender, loving care it would soon take on a new lease of life. He would easily be able to exchange his find for a few dollars or a good meal –whichever was the better bargain!

So, as you can see, eternal love doesn't last very long, does it? One glimpse of Lana – seductive, scheming, evil as hell – and it was gone! Just like that! Francis, of course, knew exactly what she was – after all, he could virtually read her mind, couldn't he? – but it did not really matter to him! He just couldn't help himself – which is why he was again at the midnight hour listening to 'Jealousy', dancing to it, hypnotized by it, loving the feel of a real, flesh-and-blood woman in his arms. While, against Lana's sun-bronzed skin, Jeannie's diamond necklace sparkled and shimmered... and the water-rats who lived in the river nipped and bit each other. Meanwhile, the altar of memory was lying abandoned amid the corruption of the refuse dump, with only a crow and an ageing tramp as unknowing witnesses to man's inconstancy.

# Blind Date

*I want all of it, now,* though Freddie Mercury phrased it better. It was exactly the way the woman named Leah saw the world. She had at times been such a naughty girl – a prostitute on the streets, a stripper working seedy, city clubs and, finally, a madam with her own profitable business that she still ran, but now in a less hands-on way. It had satisfied her always, for she had never needed a man to love – only for sex.

Recently there had been a change, for now she felt emptiness within her. Was it too late to experience this mysterious, perhaps inexplicable emotion that seemed to consume so many people, but which she had only seen as a business?

A very strange message appeared on her computer screen yesterday – from whom she had no idea, except that he called himself Christopher. His message was like a shipwreck calling from the middle of the ocean and, now that it was filling the whole of her monitor, she was bemused and mystified. She had certainly never become involved in dating sites online, never needed to be. There were great dangers and scams out there for the unwary, but here was this man addressing her by name and inviting her to dine with him. Was it perhaps fate calling her? It was certainly strange, but for some unfathomable reason she was not frightened and didn't think that someone with evil intent was trying to snare her within his web.

Her fingers with their long, painted nails hesitated for just a second, poised over the keyboard. Yes, she would accept his offer – it was too intriguing to resist: any funny business and she had plenty of nefarious contacts to protect her. Perhaps she would even take one of them to the restaurant and seat him at a corner table where he could watch over the proceedings . . . but, no, that was to lack backbone, which had never happened to her before.

Wednesday, at half past eight was the appointed time. The restaurant was middle of the road, not top quality, but then again nothing that she felt ashamed to enter. It was called Limbo, every inch of it decorated with paintings of heaven and hell. Little cherubs floating in a blue sky surveyed the diners from the walls, while from the ceiling the flames and horrors of hell looked down upon them. The woman thought it was all rather unsettling and intuited that maybe Christopher was a man with a wry, dry sense of humour. Because she didn't know her dining companion, she too decided to be middle of the road, in a smart pair of trousers, a pretty feminine blouse and a little bolero jacket; her jewellery she kept to the minimum, for there was no need to give him any clues as to how well off she was.

As she walked in, her senses were assailed by the contradictory, opposing painted scenes. Now she felt quite nervous which was not her thing at all. She looked first to the left and felt her stomach melt – this was going to be a complete pleasure she thought as her eyes were drawn towards her prospective companion, a big swarthy, dark-complexioned Adonis of a man . . . but no, he turned his face away as she smiled at him.

On the other side of the restaurant the only unaccompanied diner was a gentle-faced, youngish man who gave her a welcoming grin. A flicker of disappointment went through her – why did it have to be him, as it surely was, rather than the gorgeous, heavily-built hunk?

Christopher stood up politely and gave a slight bow. She was surprised by the deep scars on his face and by the fact that he had a couple of teeth missing – had he never thought of going to a dentist! Neither of these flaws, however, could detract from his kind expression as a strange sort of attraction drew her to him.

"Welcome, Leah, thank you for accepting my invitation. I hope it didn't upset you, because that would be the last thing in the world that I would have wanted."

He's so good-natured, she thought, but even so I don't really think he's going to be my type. Not enough oomph! I need excitement, I want life and she could hear Freddie Mercury's song echoing in her head.

"How did you find my name and my email address?"

"I know how strange this must seem, but I had to do it, Leah, and you will just have to accept this as the one and only explanation that I can offer you.

The waiter poured out a blood-red wine that somehow tasted sweet despite its strength. There followed bread, but Christopher refused butter or oil on his and simply broke it into pieces. To her surprise he offered her a thin fragment and she held out both hands, one on top of the other, to accept it, being very careful not to drop any crumbs –as though it really mattered!

As the meal of somewhat bland food

continued, Leah noticed that the companion of her dreams had somehow managed to order a spicy, very hot dish that looked and smelled absolutely wonderful – it had certainly not been on the menu because she most definitely would have chosen it!

"Tell me about yourself, Christopher. What do you do for a living?" (She might as well find out if he had a healthy bank account! That might help tip the scales in his favour, because nothing else would!)

"I'm a social worker," he replied, while Leah thought that she could well describe her own profession in exactly the same way." I've always felt it my duty to help people, for there are so many lost souls in the world."

"Oh dear, he really is a wimp – a bit of a goody-goody to say the least. What on earth would he think of me? And what a boring, boring evening this is turning out to be."

"And you, Leah? What do you do?"

She hesitated for a couple of seconds.

"Well, I'm in the men's fashion business. So very interesting, so many different tastes!" She bit her tongue at this, but continued on regardless. "I love dressing men (and undressing them too was the thought that sprang to mind!). I cater for all needs."

Christopher looked deep into her eyes.

"Yes, I can see that this might be an interesting career. But can I ask you if you have any regrets?" By this time the wine was beginning to affect her, for she gave a loud, unladylike guffaw that made the other diners look in their direction.

"No, of course not! Why should I have any regrets? It's what I'm good at. It's all fun and entertainment.

"Fun and entertainment! Surely not!"

"Oh, give it up, Leah!" she said to herself. "What a prat he is!" He would be totally shocked if only he knew her dark, little secrets. They were simply not on the same planet.

Christopher, suddenly, looked across at the gorgeous hunk of manhood that had so switched her on when she had first entered the restaurant.

"You know what, Leah; I have the distinct feeling that our little friendship is going nowhere. We just don't gel, do we? I think that you will agree."

"Yes, I'm sorry, Christopher, but, of course, you are quite right."

"I think the best I can do is to introduce you to my friend Lucius- I saw you give him an admiring look when you came in."

Leah blushed, for probably the first time in

her life – give him his due, Christopher was certainly observant.

So up he staggered and limped across to Lucius's table. He was in a bad way was poor Christopher and would be a liability for any woman – hefty health bills, a drain on time and energy – sod that for a laugh! She'd got more to do with her life than to sacrifice it for him – and what about sex, for he obviously wasn't going to be much fun in that respect, was he?

She could see him pointing her out to Lucius who stood up and came over to her. His eyes seemed to pierce her soul and although she was aroused by his sexual attraction, she knew immediately that he was not the one for her either.

There was a strange smell emanating from him of smoke and of old age – she supposed it was merely a sign that his pheromones were all wrong for her. She guessed too that he was a smoker for she could see the tell-tale yellow stains on his fingers. This was another factor that did not appeal to her, for although she possessed too many sins to count, smoking was not one of them

"Well, Leah what a pleasure to meet you finally face to face," said Lucius's dark, dark voice.

"Finally!" exclaimed Leah. "But you don't

know me, Lucius – have never heard of me!"

"Believe me, Leah, I know you very well indeed: in fact, almost too well, as indeed does Christopher."

Christopher moved away from the table and left them to it.

The world seemed to be revolving, whirling around in her mind. She simply didn't understand what was going on.

"I'm glad that you're not very keen on Christopher – it makes everything so much easier for me!"

Leah wanted to reply that she didn't care much for him either, but instead held her tongue. She sensed that it was better to keep silent, for his anger would surely be terrible to behold.

"You feel that Christopher is less than a man, don't you? But I've known him for a very, very long time and can tell you, unequivocally, that this is simply not true. I just so wish that I had listened more attentively both to him and to his father."

Suddenly flames shot down from the ceiling and she could feel suffocating heat and her skin burning.

"He is braver and better than anyone I have ever known. He suffered for three long, agonising hours, sacrificing himself for us all on a dogwood tree, with his wrists and ankles tightly bound with rope."

Leah's stomach churned and she finally understood. Why, however, had she been chosen for this experience, for she was no one special?

"Christopher," she whispered, "come back to me, help me," – but when she turned around, he had gone, although the door was still half open as though waiting for her to follow.

"I hate him, Leah, I hate his goodness, his sanctimonious words, although in my heart I know that each one is worth more than the beauty of all the stars shining in the night sky. I'm lost just as you are lost – two sinners together, but my sins, I fear, will never be absolved. But there is still time for you, a chance for you to repent. Go and find your blind date and ask for his help. And help you, he will. Put your trust in him, but don't ever trust me, although I desperately want you, desire you: for your body and especially for your soul."

The flames flickered in a state of frenzy– Lucius doubted that they would ever be extinguished, for within them there was a dark central spot of total blackness that he recognised as his soul. Nevertheless, even amid the intense heat, a chill, like a sharp dagger of ice, pierced Leah and she thought that she would die from the pain and would accompany Lucifer, for this was surely he, down into the pit of hell.

This had been the strangest blind date of all time – a tug-of-war for her affections between God and the Devil. She saw the half-open door and knew that Christopher was awaiting her, his sweetness calling to her.

The waiters and the other diners resembled wax-work figures, their faces expressionless and showing no preference for either of her suitors.

The woman named Leah was going to have it all, and would have it now, just as Freddie Mercury had sung, but not in the way that she had ever expected.

# Bocanegra

I can remember my birth as clearly as I can see into the future. I slipped out of my mother's body like a snake slithering along a jungle path after its prey. My prey was the world that I wanted so much to explore, that I couldn't possibly tarry on the way. My task, my reason for existing had to begin. Immediately everything was within my grasp and within my understanding, as it is for all of you – hidden in plain sight if you only realised it, for things are not always what they seem.

The eyes constantly deceive us – for example, there are so many more colours than the limited number that we think is available to us. The desk at which I am writing, the pen I am holding and my hand with all its muscles and blood vessels just don't, in reality, look like this at all. We are all restricted by living in a three-dimensional world that denies us seeing what is really there. Our brains and eyes are programmed to show us wonders, but it's all a mere chimera, a delusion that is tricking us and restricting our existence. I can say this, in all certainty, because from the moment I was born, it has been my privilege to have moments of true enlightenment where everything has been revealed.

The day my mother first saw me she swore there were flashes of light coming from my eyes and I know she was speaking the truth. She decided to call me Noah, saying that the name had suddenly come into her mind as though sent from spirit. She knew, from that moment, that I was different from other children. Our neighbours who lived in that lonely, wooded village used to gossip and giggle about us partly, I think, out of fear, for they could see that we were somehow strange.

I had no father. My mother always maintained that she had never been with a man so that she was mockingly called the Immaculate Virgin of Grey's Wood.

"You cannot go around telling such lies," the ageing vicar had once said to her.

"You interfering old sod," she'd whispered under her breath.

The next day he was dead, not as a result of anything she'd done, but *I* knew, full well, what had caused his demise.

I was sent to the village school, although I

needed no teaching, but I had to be seen to conform to the norms of society because, of course, it was a legal requirement. Naturally, years later, I won a scholarship to Cambridge, a completely unnecessary exercise. This was followed by a doctorate from MIT – I could have accomplished that at five years' of age, but I knew I had to endure the boredom of it all because this was what I had been told to do. My masters would not have allowed it otherwise.

I stood in front of my students in the lecture theatre listening to their sounds of awe and admiration. I had suddenly become a wizard for them, not a trickster trying to fool them: they knew me too well for that. My task was to educate these most intelligent of young people into the secrets of the universe so that our world could advance more quickly than it had ever done, for the earth was lagging far, far behind its potential and would destruct if it failed to catch up with other bodies in the great cosmos.

The charged particles of electrons, protons and neutrons spat and sparkled from my fingers like an electric storm as they whizzed and flickered through the lecture room totally amazing everyone. This was just the beginning of everything, for I would show them how to irrigate the deserts, how to keep the planet healthy and moist, and most important I would give them the key to these wonders.

Nevermore, would they be at the mercy of physics, for I could show them another way to advance our planet. Needing only to use the mind, I, Noah Bocanegra, would lead the way.

However, my scientific research has always been derided and persecuted by the great energy companies, just as other great scientists in the past. They don't after all want someone giving the world limitless free energy that will deny them the millions and billion of dollars that they can place in their greedy, corrupt bank accounts. They care not a jot for the good of the world. Their only concern is to live the life of the fat cat. The day of revelation, however, has arrived and they too have been deceived.

My masters had lied to me; the people from the constellation of Orion, with their huge, slimy, green bodies and terrifying, red eyes burning with hate, had lied to me.

It had all been a celestial joke. I was supposed to help the world they told me, but that wasn't their intention at all. My mother, that dearest of souls, was deceived too, and I hate, hate them for all that they have done.

Why I have been punished in this way I have

no idea, but I have brought the dark side of creation to a potentially wonderful planet. I can see exactly what I have done, for I am looking down upon you all from a thousand light years away and there is no lush, green foliage adorning the hills and mountains, no fruitful deserts, no fabulous curving bridges carrying what you think of as futuristic transport over amazing cities. I was mocked when they called me Noah, but the great deluge is now upon you.

I am watching the world gradually filling with blue liquid and even from this distant corner of creation I can hear through radio waves the bubbling, babbling, gushing water that is overwhelming everything. I can hear the gasping, the wheezing, the fighting for breath as lungs heave to keep body and soul alive. This time there is no Noah's Ark to help mankind and I certainly have come to the end of my useful life, so please don't look to me for aid.

I am dying, as indeed we all are, but you are merely drowning. I shall have a far worse death, for when I reach Orion, my brain will be extracted from my skull –no anaesthetic, nothing to soften the pain. That is not their way for they are the psychopaths of the universe, completely empty of empathy towards others. My spirit will be sent to some other hapless, heavenly body, again, to wreak havoc.

Because I can foretell the future, I know that my name will be Cain, the bringer of death – another sick joke to fool the inhabitants of yet another world. Thus Cain Bocanegra will open his dark mouth, and suffering and death will fall onto the innocent people of some distant sphere who at this moment have no idea of what horror is coming to them.

If any of you by some miracle survive the great flood, learn to be untrusting and cynical for, as I have already warned you, things are very rarely what they seem to be.

You're at it again, aren't you? Believing, I mean! Well, it's not as though I haven't given you plenty of warning! Brilliant scientist! Noah Bocanegra! Cain Bocanegra! Creatures with slimy, green bodies! What a load of tosh! Really… I was too thick to pass even GCE needlework. Any ideas, any scientific facts (which, by the way, I don't really understand) indeed anything of interest in this little tale, I have gleaned solely by chance while surfing the net!

Actually, I'm sitting in a deck chair on the beach at Brighton, with one eye on this piece of paper and the other on the look-out out for any gorgeous hunk who happens to pass by. My name is Jane – Jane Smith – and that is the honest truth, which I finally give you my full permission to believe!

# Conrad's War

It's a rotten old world, isn't it? Why, even Conrad, with his limited ability could see that, and be moved by what he saw; could look beyond his own little microcosm and appreciate the sadness that is all around us. Pictures of wide-eyed children, their stomachs swollen with hunger; people lying bleeding and injured; wars, famine, natural disasters; all these tragedies unfolded before his eyes on the television set in their small flat by the sea.

His mother, generally, tried to switch off the news before it came on, but, of course, these things tended to filter through, so that she would often come upon poor Conrad, with tears running down his pudding-like face, wringing his hands in anguish at what he was watching.

"They're just pictures, Conrad! Think of them as scenes from a film! They're no more real than that!"

Something, however, told Conrad that they were very real indeed.

He had never been sent away to a home – there had been no need, for there was no husband and no other children to consider, which meant that his mother could devote her whole life to him as she had done, willingly and lovingly, for the last twenty-five years.

What Conrad needed at that moment, she decided, was a little outing down to the beach to cheer him up, for they couldn't see the sea from their flat and she knew that he missed it – in fact, their only view was a car showroom and the front of a supermarket. He was delicate and there had been such a strong wind blowing through the little sea-side town during the last fortnight that she had forbidden him to leave the house.

Now, at last, it looked as though summer might have decided to make an entrance onto the stage; the sun was shining down upon the world like a spotlight, the wind had made a final, dramatic exit and everyone could feel warm air waiting in the wings. Yes, today Conrad could finally take the little bus down to the seashore.

So, he trotted happily into his bedroom to fetch the little wicker basket that he took everywhere whenever he left the house. He tucked into the bottom of it his precious collection of toy soldiers; the first time ever that he had decided to take them with him on one of his little outings. They were so beautifully painted – it had taken him hours, days, months of painstaking effort to achieve this perfection: sitting with his brows furrowed, his tongue protruding from the side of his mouth in concentration, as he'd delicately wielded the small brush. His eyesight wasn't good, hence the thick pebble glasses that he wore, and his hands had always been rather unsteady and looked as though they were far too big and beefy for such intricate work, so that the result was all the more impressive.

Now, lovingly wrapped in a gingham napkin to prevent any possible damage, the troop of soldiers awaited their first, real military exercise. On top of his little army his mother placed a Tupperware box full of his favourite sugar sandwiches and a thermos of milky coffee. As for Conrad himself, he was, as usual, immaculately turned out – she always saw to that – trousers smartly pressed, shoes gleaming, shirt snow-white and his jumper fluffy and bobble-free.

"Come on, Conrad, time for the bus! …Are you sure you should be taking your soldiers? Just don't lose any of them, that's all! What would you do then?"

Of course, he wanted to take them, for they were going to be on duty, defending the castle that he would build for them on the sand. So, carrying his wicker basket in one hand and, in the other, a supermarket bag, inside which lay his favourite bright red bucket and spade, they made their way along the street, over the pedestrian crossing and so to the bus stop.

His mother put him on the bus and handed his fare over to the driver. This would be one of the few times when she'd allowed him to go by himself, but the beach was only ten minutes away and he knew which bus stop would bring him home again. With his return ticket safely in his anorak pocket, he waved at her excitedly as the bus moved off.

Half-an-hour later, she was booked-in for a hospital appointment that she couldn't talk to him about, for he simply would not have understood, and she didn't want him to understand: a little lump that shouldn't have been there.

Tommy and Spike were supposed to have been at school but, as so often happened, had decided to play truant. The weather was too good to be wasted in some boring, old classroom, so they had slung their hoodies around their waists and placed their baseball caps back to front on their heads. Now they felt like the real McCoy as they sauntered along the esplanade, hands in their jeans' pockets, their eyes covered by shades that they hoped made them look cool and rather sinister – two twelve- year-old boys, rebellious, restless and looking for trouble.

Conrad, sat happily by himself on the beach – it was too early for the tourist season and most people were at work at that hour, so that the wide stretch of sand and pebble was totally at his disposal: he was truly master of all he surveyed. He had lined his soldiers up in smart formations, so that they already seemed to be performing sentry duty; keeping out any potential intruders, while the delicate task of building the castle was being carried out.

Meticulous as he was in everything, Conrad manoeuvred, shaped and brought the sand under his control like a potter with his clay.

Unfortunately, the resulting castle was not the picture of perfection that he imagined it to be, but what did that matter? He thought it was wonderful. So, from his wicker basket, he then took out some little flags that he had asked his mother to purchase at the newsagents to complete the beauty of its construction.

Over the moat, through the bailey, up to the keep and into the towers marched the soldiers, their red and blue uniforms complementing wonderfully the colours of the little flags, which were now moving in the breeze – it was a sight of which to be truly proud and a strange emotion stirred within Conrad's simple heart. Finally, the soldiers were doing what they had been created to do and standing where they were meant to stand: some facing inland; others keeping a careful watch for marauders coming from over the vast expanse of the sea.

Thirsty and hungry from all the unaccustomed fresh air and from the efforts of his labours, Conrad sipped his milky coffee and, then, took his first bite of his delicious sugar sandwiches – he just loved the crunchy sensation of all that sweetness between his teeth, with its buttery accompaniment melting onto his tongue.

What a perfect morning it had been for him: sun, sea, sand; a wonderful castle with all its fine troops on duty; sugar sandwiches and milky coffee – such is the deserving paradise for an innocent soul like Conrad.

However, the black kiss of misfortune was about to alight upon his lips, the convergence of the Titanic with the iceberg – in other words trouble was on its way!

Tommy and Spike, only just an hour into their saunter by the sea, were already beginning to wonder if perhaps it might have been more fun to go to school; then they suddenly spied on the beach a solitary figure with what looked like a sizeable box of edible goodies at hand. Having failed to have breakfast and feeling decidedly peckish, they agreed to go and investigate. Over the railings of the esplanade they leaned, frightening poor Conrad half to death, for he was a bit deaf and hadn't heard their approach,

"Hey, mate, what you got there, then?" yelled Spike. "Give us a sarnie!"

Conrad wondered why the boy hadn't asked nicely with a please, but nevertheless, with his Tupperware box in his hand, he walked over the pebbles and politely offered it up to them. Tommy was the first to take a bite and immediately spat it out onto the road. "What the 'ell's this then? Sugar sarnies… you some sort of nutter or what? Bleedin' 'ell, you've got to 'ave something better than this."

Spike grinned. "Let's do a bit of investigatin', shall we, Tommy?"

It had only taken a second to see that Conrad was a few sandwiches short of a picnic, so over the railings they'd climbed and down onto the beach. This is what they liked to see – someone weaker than themselves, someone whom they could taunt, and someone whom they could knock around a bit if they felt like it: in other words, an outlet for all their pent-up energy. Conrad looked like the ideal victim.

"What's your name then? …Conrad! Conrad! You've got to be jokin' …never heard that one before! 'Ave you Spike? Ever 'eard of a Conrad?"

"Naah, never heard that before…! Got any money on you, Conrad? … Look, Tommy a bus ticket – I reckon 'is mum must've given 'im just the correct money for 'is bus fare, with nothing left over for us. That right, Conrad?"

Conrad nodded his head in agreement.

Tommy, in the meantime, had wandered over to the sandcastle.

"Mummy's little boy making sandcastles, is 'e….? Ooh…. and toy soldiers! They're pretty aren't they, Spike?... Look, look, Conrad, pretty, pretty toy soldiers for a pretty, pretty boy!" Tommy said as he picked up one of the precious, red-coated, little soldiers that Conrad had spent so much time painting and held it in front of Conrad's face.

"Don't touch!" Conrad said.

"What was that you said, Conrad? Don't touch! Giving orders now, are you? Well, we'll see about that."

Tommy and Spike looked at each other, winked and then went around collecting each of the soldiers before depositing the whole collection at Conrad's feet.

"Well," said Tommy, "there's no one standing guard over the castle now, Conrad, so we can do what we like with it, can't we? There's no one going to attack us now, is there?" …So, they stamped on the castle and jumped on it and, using Conrad's favourite red spade to help them, razed the whole edifice to the ground as though it had never existed, the beautiful flags now torn and broken.

By this time, Conrad was on his knees sobbing for what they had done to his lovely castle. This was just the beginning of his nightmare, however, for now they turned their attention to the soldiers. They emptied his little wicker basket and into it dropped all those wonderfully uniformed military figures, the most prized of all his possessions. Crying out, poor Conrad tried to grab hold of the basket, but Tommy kicked him in the face, took his hoodie from his waist, placing it instead around Conrad's neck so that he couldn't move. Spike, meanwhile, went to the edge of the beach and walked until he was thigh-deep in water, which was as far as he dared go. Then, all at once, he upturned the basket, allowing all the soldiers to float away on top of the waves, the seagulls' raucous screeching sounding like a fanfare to herald their one and only naval battle. It was now Spike's turn to kick Conrad, this time in the stomach, but the novelty of the attack was wearing off by now, plus the fact that they were both probably feeling a bit nervous of the repercussions should they ever be identified and caught – after all, they had assaulted a grown man and they knew from watching television that you didn't get away scot-free for doing something like that.

"Okay, Conrad, you got off lightly this time. Just remember, if you meet us again don't ever try to give us orders because you know now the sort of thing that might 'appen to you."

Nevertheless, there was just one final gesture of sheer viciousness to bring down the curtain on their cruelty; Spike removed Conrad's pebble glasses, broke them in two and crunched them under his heavy trainers. Now Conrad was totally helpless.

With that, Tommy grabbed his hoodie and they disappeared along the sea front in the direction of the fun fair where they could perhaps create more mischief, but it wouldn't be as much fun as they had just had. Yes, they'd certainly proved themselves to be the real McCoy alright, certainly frightened the crap out of old Conrad!

Fate, however, sometimes has a way of sorting out questions of right and wrong, with no intervention needed from the law: and so it was with Tommy and Spike as they walked towards the fun-fair, totally unfocused on anything except fooling around and playfully punching each other. At 12:46 precisely, a white van with Jacob's Fun-fair written in large red letters on its side, careered into them, the driver too occupied with reading a text message to notice them until their bodies were flung against the windscreen. An hour later the hospital pathologist removed from the pockets of their torn, blood-soaked hoodies a couple of beautifully painted toy soldiers that would now never again stand to attention or sail with their comrades

At about the same time, bewildered, blindly helpless, utterly traumatised, Conrad was found by the police cowering against the sea wall, his poor face a mass of bruises. In his simple mind he wondered what great wrong he must have done to bring on this terrible, terrible punishment – neither he nor his soldiers had harmed anyone, not like the awful things that he saw people on television do to each other.

No-one quite knew what had happened to him that day, for he could never be persuaded to say much about it, but he certainly refused ever to go anywhere near the beach again. He just hoped that his little regiment, wherever it had ended up, was happy; and he wept at the thought of its loss. "Yours was the most smartly-dressed, colourful army in the whole wide world," his mother said, and she wept with him.

Six months later Conrad had to go into a home, for his mother was no longer there to look after him.

It's a rotten old world, isn't it?

# Exposure Time

He was not the product of any virgin birth that was for sure, so who had sown the seed that started off the miracle of his existence? Any questions he had ever asked about his father had produced eruptions of such seismic proportions that he had been afraid to delve further. He'd searched the house from top to bottom, but had never found any documents, letters or photos to help him.

His elderly kin were equally reticent on the subject, never dropping the slightest hint. It was too late to learn the truth from his mother, for she was now living a senile existence, her secrets forever locked in some deep place within her muddled collection of brain cells.

She still lived at home with a weekly visit from a specialist, Dr. Carlson, but there wasn't anything he could do for her. It just cost the family a substantial amount of money to listen to his useless advice. They were unwilling to put her in a home, for they were of a social class that existed quite happily with battiness and eccentricity. Mother virtually had a wing of the imposing house to herself with, of course, a full-time carer – no changing of soiled nappies and the preparation of slops by her loving family. Who could blame them, for they had plenty of money and would have even more when mother kicked the bucket?

Serena looked closely into Joshua's eyes, wondering about him, because she could sense that the older he became the more troubled he was by the mystery; a forty-year-old man who desperately wanted to know about his father. Nevertheless, perhaps some things were better hidden forever. He had begun to have very unsettling dreams that were repeated over and over again. Waking up sweating and shaking, he knew that something was nudging the edge of his memory, but nothing made sense and he could never quite remember what he had seen. Sometimes he thought there was a man dressed in red, but he could never get beyond that; it was certainly not Father Christmas: this figure was too menacing to be bringing gifts.

 The next time Dr. Carlson came to see mother, Serena mentioned Joshua's dreams, but he already knew about them, and suggested they were probably manifestations of his fear of growing older. Mid-life crisis time had finally arrived for Joshua!

"Just forget about it, Serena, and tell Joshua to do the same. Self-doubt and too much self-absorption – that's his problem. He needs something outside himself to keep him occupied." Laughing, he added, "Perhaps he should find himself a little bit of stuff, something on the side – that would certainly buck him up!"

Serena was shocked that the specialist should suggest anything so outrageous and certainly didn't find the idea at all amusing. She decided not to tell Joshua any of this – you never knew what strange ideas men of a certain age might get into their heads. The fact that she herself was searching through online dating agencies was her own little secret, she doubted if she would actually do anything about it.

Dr. Carlson, although he knew there were a couple of decades between them, had been seriously turned on by Serena from the first moment that he'd set eyes on her. She was a true beauty, married to dull, boring Joshua gripped by his obsession to find his father, but for some lucky, lucky man she would make a very rich wife: if only her husband could be removed from the land of the living. All doctors always had a cupboard-full of lethal drugs to hand, and could be walking, talking killing machines if they played their cards right. He had lately begun to consider this idea seriously and would definitely continue to do so.

Serena went into the sitting room where Joshua was slumbering in his usual armchair.

He was in one of his frequently-visited dream worlds, desperately trying to reach the house where he had been born and brought up, but however much he tried he never arrived there. It was such a long walk and on the way he always passed through a pair of factory gates and, trembling, descended the stone steps into the main building, but had a hell of a job finding the way out again so that he could continue his trek. He just wanted to find his parents, to have his mother's arms around him, but his father remained obscure. He was now passing through a council estate where most people seemed to take great pride in the appearance of their houses as though there were trophies for the smartest. He knew that he would next arrive in the middle of a city and be fascinated by the big department stores, although he intuited that this scene was nothing to do with what he had experienced. Then he would suddenly find himself going down a gentle, grassy slope, the evening gloom gathering about him.

To reach his home it seemed it always had to be night time and as he approached would first see the wonderful Norman abbey, full of light, outside and inside – sometimes he would go inside, but never, never would he go up the stone steps of the tower. Again, it was not as it was in real life. The abbey of his dreams was larger and stood at a different angle from the main road. He hadn't far to go now, but he would never reach his destination – that was always to be outside his grasp.

Was it because he didn't really want to arrive?

There was some reason for the failure and thus he would always wake up at this point, frustrated and agitated.

He knew that he only had to go to another part of the house to have his mother's arms again around him, but he would be a stranger to her, a strange man innocently wanting to place his head on her breast and breathe in the perfume that it seemed she had worn forever. His father, however, was a different matter, an unknown figure hovering on the edge of reality, who seemed destined to remain there.

Dr. Carlson, in other words, Joshua's father, as I'm

sure you've already guessed – no sting in the tail with this story, I'm afraid – didn't, in his heart, want to kill his own son, but it was either that or lose any hope of marrying the glorious Serena with all the millions she would inherit. His only doubt was that perhaps she might reject him which would be something of a disaster for him and very unwise for her.

He needn't have worried, however, because Joshua was going to stop him in his tracks, so the problem wouldn't arise.

The Doctor had a real penchant for murder, and he really enjoyed committing this most heinous of sins. He thought that this would be murder number five, but perhaps his memory was deceiving him. He was probably going the same way as poor, mindless Cynthia, Joshua's mother, who had not remembered him at all, of course. Well, that phase of his life had happened a long time ago and the marriage had lasted only seven years, ending in the dramatic scenes now lurking deep in Joshua's mind.

Anyway, he had changed his name several times and thought himself well and truly safe. He'd made an amazing amount of money from the last wills and testaments of many of his patients, but *much* always wants *more,* doesn't it?

Nevertheless, exposure time was fast

approaching and Joshua's subconscious was rising to the surface, ready to reveal its secrets.

A couple of days later, again slumbering in front of the television, he awoke screaming at the top of his voice, the television football commentary completely drowned by the noise. He'd seen it all. He now understood everything.

Serena nearly jumped out of her skin. "For God sake, Joshua, can't you ever get out of that damned chair? I'm so bored with you! You live in a constant trough of self-pity. Make some effort and go and look for your bloody father if you're so anxious to find him."

He listened to her ranting and raving, but he didn't need to go anywhere now, for the enigma was solved and he would sort his father out well and truly . . . the bastard!

*The fierce man in a red robe with a wig on his head had allowed him to give his evidence from the body of the courtroom, rather than place him in the witness stand. He was, after all, just a frightened, little boy at a murder trial and had to be treated as gently as possible. They needed to hear what his childish voice had to say, for he had been the sole witness to the crime. He had watched his father killing his mother's sister for whom he lusted, but she'd rejected him, which he could not possibly allow. She had to be punished for her insubordination, and one night the little boy, creeping out of his bedroom, to fetch a glass of water, watched it all from the gloom of the landing. His father had grabbed her by the neck and thrown her down the steep stairway, her back broke as it hit the last step. Joshua heard his father's contemptuous laughter and the foul words he uttered. The jury sat with tears in their eyes and the silence in the vast court of justice had been palpable, as the frail little soul told his terrible tale.*

*Nevertheless, fate takes its own course and Dr Carlson's luck was with him. A five-year sentence was his paltry punishment. Needless to say, the newspapers and the public were in an uproar at what they considered to be a travesty of justice. The only consolation was that poor, pale Joshua who had seen so much horror in his short life was protected by his own mind which forgot what had happened. His mother took him abroad for a few years, hoping that the horrendous experience would remain forever locked in his subconscious.*

Down the stairs tumbled Dr. Carlson, battered and bruised by the treatment his son had inflicted upon him. He lay dead and lifeless at Joshua's feet; a pity really because he'd escaped again the punishment he deserved, but perhaps, in another world, he would pay for everything he'd done.

Serena placed her arm around Joshua's waist, put her head on his shoulder and kissed him. Whatever happened, she would support him and be at his side.

As they stood there entwined, they heard the police sirens approaching and Serena just had to have faith that the law would understand and that Lady Justice would take off her blindfold of impartiality and see things as they truly were.

# Fertility

Well, the funeral was over, the will had been read and much good had it done her, damn it! For so long she had lived in the sure and certain hope of her reward, but, as things had turned out, absolutely to no avail. So much effort and all for nothing! Poor Bella!

So, there she sat, the photo albums strewn around at her feet, the poodle puppy dozing on the arm of her chair, the fire blazing nicely as dusk fell, and a strong whiskey and soda on the small table beside her.

It had been a difficult day; the church, the graveside, the wake and all those black clothes. The most difficult part of all, of course, had been trying to contain her excitement, her anticipation of what the solicitor would surely have in store for her; trying to look sad, trying very hard not to rub her hands in glee. The lowering of the coffin into the damp earth had meant that her mission was finally accomplished. At that point she'd had to cover her mouth to stifle the giggles that were threatening to bubble to the surface... All for nought, however! Her bloody father! The wicked old devil!

What a fertile family they had been. In fact, too much fertility for their own good! Three elder brothers, one older sister – not forgetting cousins galore, though they, of course, hadn't counted in the inheritance stakes! She'd once heard someone say that without a family, you're just a shadow passing – what she wouldn't have given to be such a shadow – it would have saved so much trouble.

She bent forward, picked up one of the photo albums and idly turned over the pages. Freddy on the beach! In a striped bathing suit, no less! What a sight, but then he'd never been much to look at, had he? Fortunately, she and her other siblings had fared better. Freddy, however – well, she'd sometimes wondered if he'd had a different father from the rest of them. After all, mother, so rumours went, had been a bit of a goer in her younger days and perhaps Freddy had been living proof of this. Anyway, it didn't matter now, for he was long dead and buried – the first one that she'd seen off, for she had been quite meticulous in disposing of them all in strict chronological order. He'd actually been a bit of an experiment, had Freddy, her first foray into the realms of murder – well, homicide to be more accurate because she had already successfully disposed of various family pets – really just to get the feel of the thing – nothing personal!

Foxgloves are such pretty flowers, aren't they, with their lovely pink bells …and so very, very useful when you have murder in mind – digitalis is the name of the game when you want a nice, simple, easily overlooked death. There's no need to hurry with digitalis. You can just take your time …and, of course, it is so much more interesting that way. Yes, a particularly useful flower, the foxglove. Especially, of course, if, like Bella, you're on intimate – well, very intimate terms – with the local doctor. No problems at all there, when it came to obtaining a death certificate; for Freddy, for James, for Cynthia, for Alan and finally for Father! All victims of that wondrous drug digitalis – so easy to procure, so easy to administer!

Bella turned to the next page of the photo album and there was Cynthia simpering in her angel costume at the nativity play. How Bella had envied her – the wonderful white feathery wings, the white silk dress and most of all the silver halo wobbling about rather unsteadily on Cynthia's pretty, blonde curls. In the background stood the three shepherds, frozen in time at the very instant in which Alan was about to bring his crook down upon James's head. The third, diminutive shepherd, Bella, was caught with her mouth open, gazing wide-eyed in horror, at the assault!

Those had been such happy days, the innocence of childhood; before their mother's death, long before thoughts of greed and murder had entered her head. She sometimes wondered what had turned her into a killer; pure greed, a rogue gene or was it simply because she was just evil, a servant of the devil? Poor Bella!

At the end of the funeral wake the chosen few had remained behind in the drawing room – cousin George and his pale-faced little wife, Uncle Cedric, red-faced and pot-bellied, Aunt Maud and her silly son Simon: in other words, those who would receive meaningless, paltry, insignificant mementos from the estate. Hers would be the prize; all of it, every lovely penny of it. What she had worked for, planned for! It was not, however, until the solicitor's gaze strayed over his half glasses and over her left shoulder that she realised that their number had grown; a woman with flame-coloured hair and scarlet lipstick, a handsome blonde, teenaged boy and a pretty little girl of about ten years old! In other words, Father's legitimate, legal, absolutely inheritance-proof second family! Once again fertility had reared its ugly head! Poor Bella!

There was no way, however, that she was going to be able rid the world of those pestilent usurpers, that rotten little family that had dashed her hopes to pieces. She was just too tired, too eaten up with disappointment to have the energy to do anything about them. She would simply leave the foxgloves to grow unmolested, which is perhaps what she should have done in the first place, but there had been a real, deep satisfaction as she'd seen them all dying one by one. "No, admit defeat, Bella," she said to herself. "Your killing days are well and truly over!"

The fire was dying, the poodle had woken from his slumbers and whiskey, well, several whiskies in fact, had disappeared down Bella's throat. She didn't feel at all well and her left arm was beginning to ache, so she irritably kicked the photo albums across the carpet. She supposed she'd better get up and take the poodle out into the garden and make sure that he spent a penny, because she certainly didn't want to hear him barking and scratching at the bedroom door in the middle of the night asking to go out.

She suddenly felt a terrible pain in her chest. A heart attack, that's what it must certainly be, she thought! She stood up, trying to breathe deeply and to cough deeply which she knew was what one was supposed to do in this event, but she simply couldn't manage it; the pain was too intense. For the first time ever there was no doctor when she needed one! Ironic, wasn't it?

Even at this late stage, however, there was to be one more death added to her list of victims, probably the most innocent and harmless of them all. Yes, Bella remained a killer even as she died, for she was a big woman and when her heavy body landed on the small black poodle who was gazing anxiously up at her, he died almost instantly, his breath literally knocked out of his tiny body.

So, as you can see, what with one thing and another, it just hadn't been her day, had it? Poor Bella!

# Grey World

Regretting it forever, I unwillingly caught sight of them all, sitting in their serried ranks. Not a finger twitched, not an eye blinked, not a muscle moved: they might as well have been waxen figures staring unseeingly into the distance. What they saw was a mystery to me and to anyone else unfortunate enough to be there. My nostrils were assailed with the smell of old age, of unwashed bodies, of soiled clothes.

Greyness was the overwhelming colour before me: grey motionless beings in grey dresses, grey tangled hair hanging loosely around grey expressionless faces. It was like looking at the epitome of death where at any moment they would cease to exist and the undertaker would rush in to perform his duties, bringing with him the only sign of life.

Their backs were as stiff as ram rods, giving a sense that at any moment they might collapse and disintegrate into nothing. They could well have remained like that for eternity.

I had come upon them by an accident of fate, having really intended only a quick chat and a cup of tea with the staff. I had wanted my introduction to her to be slow so that I could acclimatise myself gradually to her presence. I had certainly not wanted this sudden, overwhelmingly unforgettable tableau that was presented to my shocked eyes. I was utterly dismayed at my discovery, for this was madness at its grimmest. Ghostly figures in grubby white uniforms flitted amongst them trying to prise open their lips so that they might receive the unappetising slop presented to them on the dirty, food-encrusted spoons. They were obviously not going to be allowed to depart this earth before their allotted time.

Never, however, judge a book by its cover and never believe that you have seen the worst of things, for there is often far worse to follow. So it proved to be in this grey hellhole.

The old girl at the end of the second row was the most gentle-looking of the bunch, but mentally she was far, far away: fifty years back in the past, lying with her legs wide open, while the gorgeous rake of her village had his very, very wicked way with her. Her beautiful auburn hair had shone with health and her skin with the texture of peaches and cream. In other words, she had been totally gorgeous. It was also fifty years ago when her rake had left her like some piece of garbage in the gutter – and for what? For a raven-haired trollop with not an intelligent thought in her empty head!

Memories of this black beauty still irritated her to death for in her wizened, grey body the desire for vengeance continued to burn strong. The matron pointed her out to me.

Someone, in the meanwhile, was for the umpteenth time trying to shove the revolting food into her mouth. She so disliked the badly cooked, past-its-sell-by-date, half-rotten morsel that she finally snapped and bit down hard on the hand that was feeding her, for which infraction she received a hard slap on the face. It was, however, in her heart that the rage finally burst forth, the desolation of half a century reaching its climax.

She knew what she was going to do for it had been carefully planned, but unfortunately her confused mind had made a terrible mistake. The bitch who had taken away her loved one had died years ago, but in her imagination any one of her grey companions would have filled the bill and would, moreover, pay for what had been done. Suddenly her normally immobile fingers began to twitch, her elbow to bend. Searching up the sleeve of her woollen jumper she found her chosen weapon – a grim, filthy, excrement-covered gun attached to her arm by an obviously very old and frayed piece of rope.

How on earth this old dear living in a shabby home for those about to depart from this world had come in possession of such an unlikely object was anyone's guess . . . and how on earth had she single-handed managed to tie it to her arm? Had it been found under a tree, in a smelly dustbin or had she herself been keeping it hidden for all those years? How could anyone possibly ever know these imponderables?

The police slipped and slithered in the blood of the ten victims who that day went to meet their maker, while the murderess her face still immobile, laughed and giggled within, as her heart and mind rejoiced knowing that she had achieved her aim.

Revenge was, of course, the name of the game.

The other old girls trembled with shock and twittered to themselves like birds at the frightful sight, not to each other for their minds were always isolated, living in their own mute little worlds.

"It was me!" The words issued from between her dirty, yellowing, gritted teeth, blown into the air by the putrid smell of her breath. "It was me!"

Her voice croaked eerily as though it were that of a ghost, allowed finally to speak for the first time in years. As her face was splattered with blood, the police had already sussed this one out, especially as she was gripping firmly onto a gun and had managed to stand creakily on her wavering legs to better view her victims!

"You bitch!" she whispered. "Did you really think you wouldn't pay for what you did to me?"

The policemen, gently and kindly, took her by the elbows, while a WPC wrapped a blanket around her thin shoulders.

The slaughterer's name was Maudie, her mind had been always rather frail, indeed simple, but now it was as though the Devil had finally decided fully to take over her soul: hence the diabolical scene that was before us. She was entering into the dream world where she often dwelled. She could feel her swelling womb; she could feel in her arms the tiny creature swathed in a woollen blanket that must surely be hers.

She had just enough intelligence left to associate these two facts with the glorious man to whom she had given herself all those years ago, although it might as well have been yesterday, for time no longer had any meaning for her. Now that her lips had once again been loosened after so much silence, it was as though a never-ending stream of senseless babble had been released.

The WPC held her hand and stroked it soothingly. Maudie knew what she had done. "Will I hang? Will I go to hell? And my child – what of her? Will she ever know what I have done? I meant to kill, I wanted to kill, and it's what has given my life purpose all these years. Will I ever be forgiven? I wouldn't think so, would you? Would you forgive me, lady police-woman? And what do you gentlemen of the police force think of me? Something that's crawled out of a sewer, I dare say!"

She laughed and cackled like a witch, emitting a great spray of froth from her mouth. Her heart began to pump blood through her veins at a great pace, a loud pounding filling her ears so fast that her body was unable to cope.

Thus, she died and, devastated, I watched her last moments, my mother's final breath.

I was appalled. Why had destiny made me be present on this particular day? However, it was my own fault; my father had warned me not to come, but how could I not, having discovered after so many years that she was here?

He sat on the park bench perched on the hill

that looked down upon the home. He was dressed in his warm, grey overcoat for it was a bleak, windy day, the tears that flowed down his face reflecting the sad, sad, grey shadow world in which he lived and which now, after the events of yesterday, had grown even darker.

"I told you to keep away, Julia. I wish to God I hadn't ever mentioned her. She was there only for my pleasure, an object of my lust."

I was embarrassed to be talking in this vein with my own father; he'd been a dark horse, a very dark horse indeed. To his credit, he'd always taken care of me, but it had only been during the last few months that he'd told me all about my mother and her whereabouts.

In the distance over the damp hills that surrounded the ancient church, ten shadowy figures disappeared slowly into emptiness. The bell tolled and the priest intoned the centuries' old words that had served for the burial of both kings and peasants as the grey, watery skies shed their load.

After my father had sprinkled the earth onto Maudie's coffin, silence reigned again and the WPC again took on her role of comforter, wiping the tears from my eyes.

# Henry

The microphone boomed and screeched, deafening the crowd with its appalling noise. They never ever get it right – somewhere, surely, there must be a sound technician who could do it properly. Especially this year with such a very important person coming to open the fête! But no, the vicar and his so-called steering committee had botched it up, as usual!

The president of the Women's Union, however, carries on manfully … (an apt turn of phrase for such a macho, masculine woman). Twittering and simpering in a surprisingly feminine fashion she makes the eagerly awaited announcement.

"And so, it is with the greatest pleasure that I welcome our own dear Henry Faulkner to open this fête."

The crowd was puzzled – where was Henry? Surely he should have been on the little platform with all the dignitaries. Suddenly, however, everyone became aware of a tremor of excitement from the back of the crowd. People stepped aside to allow access and smiled when they recognised the famous figure moving through their midst, but he appeared to be was oblivious to everything going on around him. As he wandered across the lawn, Henry's fine aesthetic face was deep in thought, his mind obviously on higher things.

This was nonsense, of course, because Henry was always conscious of his audience and everything he did was studied and stage-managed down to the finest detail. No gesture, no facial expression, no utterance was ever left to chance… and he was, of course, master of the grand entrance. The crowd felt that they knew him like a member of their own family. After all he was in their living rooms most evenings – if only on their plasma television sets. They wanted to touch him, to call him by his first name, to tell him how much they enjoyed his work, but his distracted, distant look prevented this and they would have dared to address him only as Mr Faulkner, if at all. Soon, however, now that the Queen's Birthday Honours List had been announced, he would be Sir Henry – and why not, indeed? Hamlet, Lear, Prospero – he had played the lot! Also, Dean Strickland, of course; especially, Dean Strickland, Chief Inspector and super sleuth of the Met whose adventures the country followed avidly twice a week, with a special two-hour long episode on Sunday evenings! It was rumoured that even in Buckingham Palace, dinner on Sunday evenings was always an informal affair in front of the telly!

Today, Henry was in full Lord Byron mode – his face framed by dark curls, his white shirt frilled and a touch of pale make-up on his aquiline face with a smudge of purple under the eyes – he did, however, stop just short of giving a consumptive cough!

I watched all this from the side-line, more specifically from the entrance to the refreshment tent, where I was manning the tea urn. In fact, I was more than glad not to be among the excited throng milling around the great idol. Henry Falkner, to be honest, gave me the creeps – it always amazes me that people could find all that posturing and posing so appealing. I doubted that he had a sincere emotion in his body. Cynical, aren't I? But that's how things are with me…

Suddenly the deep baritone voice of the great actor was heard, slightly broken with emotion, of course; such were his deep feelings for the honour bestowed upon him this afternoon. To be invited to open the fête of the village where he had spent so many happy hours filming – what greater joy could there be?

If you look him up on Wikipedia, which most of us have done, you will find a fleeting mention of his marriage to Letitia Gore-Greene. It lasted but a couple of years – not because he belongs to the Pink Brigade which his appearance this afternoon might have led one to believe, but actually because he distributes his favours rather too liberally amongst anything in a skirt! Poor Letitia, a pale ethereal-looking creature, who drags herself around the concert halls of the world, literally playing second fiddle with the Parthenon Symphony Orchestra which, like everything else Greek, is about to come to a penniless, sticky end. I happen to know from an extremely reliable source that when that happens she will, again, pull out all the stops and, again, fling herself at Henry's feet knowing that he will, again, bail her out of trouble.

Well, looking around, it seems that we are finally just about ready for the great tea ceremony – cucumber sandwiches, naturally, to the fore (rather curly at the edges, but still very acceptable) created, of course, by yours truly. By the way, a word of warning! I really would think twice before digging into Mrs Swathe's tuna offerings... Their age and provenance are somewhat questionable – especially as she is suffering from one her awful runny colds!

"He's coming! He's coming! I'll just die if he looks at me. And if he speaks to me – well, at least I'll die happy!" This from silly, frothy-brained Myrtle from the Cut-Quick Hair Salon.

In they all trouped and out came the champagne – hopefully not paid for out of the church funds or, at this rate, the stained-glass window would never be repaired. So, I was for the moment rather "de trop" as they say – well, would you want tea when there's bubbly to be had!

It was at this point that Henry's popularity ratings really soared, for as soon as he received his glass of champagne he passed it on to Janey who was about to serve him with a tuna sandwich – lucky escape there, Henry! Before the steering committee could say "to be or not to be" all the helpers, except me, had been handed a glass and were standing there quaffing Veuve Clicquot.

"Don't you just love him? He's so sweet. I'd just like to take him home and give him a cuddle."

This from Mrs Barber of the Parish Council – silly old biddy! No, I'm afraid it's the gorgeous, devil-may-care Nigel Ratherton, from the next village who's my kind of man!

Then, suddenly, everyone's gaze turned in my

direction as Henry, one eyebrow quizzically lifted, slowly and rather magnificently sauntered over holding out a glass of champers towards me. Rather in the same way that Chief Inspector Dean Strickland shows his hapless victim the incriminating evidence that's going to send him to his doom!

"Ooh, Maggie, look he's going to give you a glass of champagne. I told you should have had your hair cut! If you played your cards right, you could end up being Lady Falkner. He likes them young, so I've heard."

"Don't be so silly. Who in their right mind would want to end up with him?"

So, larger than life, up comes Henry and looks straight into my eyes, well bores into them really. Not a flicker of a smile, not a hint of emotion, not a word passing his lips! Well, there wouldn't be, would there? Our little secret! After all, as he told me years ago, I'm nothing to be proud of! Daddy dear, father mine!!

As for the unfortunate Letitia! Well, everyone always says to her," Keep fiddling for as long as you possibly can, dear!" Poor mummy!

# Her Name was Aphrodite

October the fourth in the year two thousand and three at a quarter to five; it was imposed for ever in her mind and in her heart. How could Lilith ever forget, for it was the time and date when Luke, the only love of her life, had passed into a better world? There would never be anyone else to replace him and she could confidently say this after fourteen years without him.

Lilith had stayed in the clinic day and night for two months and, when he died, she had opened the window wide so that his spirit could fly unhindered to its destination. She just hoped and prayed that when her time came, he would come to meet her and that she would not have to wander aimlessly through eternity looking for him. Strangely enough she didn't often dream of Luke and when she did, she would usually search for him in vain, running through woodlands, running through passageways, upstairs, downstairs, every which way, but never managing to catch sight of him. Occasionally she did see him on the other side of a road when, for some strange reason, he would just look through her, but she never felt hurt by this rejection, being so happy just to have seen him. Very, very occasionally they would be standing side by side looking down from a hillside upon a newly built house in the little valley and that was paradise, for it presaged a life together and they would speak to each other. What heaven was that!

Why, only the night before she seen him at the end of the fabled tunnel silhouetted against a brilliant light, but something or someone had stopped her as she'd hurried towards him, her heart bursting with happiness. It was a love that was going endure for eternity. Lilith and Luke together forever!

What a glorious wedding Evie and Ezra had – the climax of a whirlwind romance. Hormones were whirling around, and lust was at its height. As for love, well, they certainly thought that they were Antony and Cleopatra, not Romeo and Juliet: age was against them for that little idyll. Yes, they were madly in love – whatever love is, as someone very much in the public eye had once so famously remarked. They had both been addicted to hard partying and all the fumbling and indiscretions that this involved. Word in the street and in their workplace was that they did, indeed, live life in the fast lane; they were your genuine swingers!

Only a month after the wedding had come and gone and the honeymoon weekend in Tuscany over and done with, the house of cards came tumbling down.

"You're a piece of scum, Ezra! Why don't you sod off home to your mummy?" screamed Lilith as she flung a kitchen knife at him, careful to avoid stabbing him – he wasn't worth a place in a prison cell.

She really did want him to go and, without any doubt at all, would tomorrow start divorce proceedings. It would, at least, give all their friends and acquaintances the most wonderful opportunity for gossip.

The marriage had barely made it beyond the wedding night, for they had both realised almost immediately that the gilt had gone off the gingerbread and that neither of them was made for commitment. It was never going to work. A pound to a penny they would soon be seeking solace elsewhere, even with each other once there was nothing legal about their arrangement – so much more fun that way.

At least, Evie had had the excitement of

choosing her very expensive and glamorous, pale pink wedding dress – pure white had been ruled out because it would have been the source of too many winks and nudges. This had been accompanied by a rather natty fascinator instead of a veil which she was sure she would wear again on some future occasion.

Ezra would certainly not be going home to his mummy, the old bag. No, he'd take himself off to the Caribbean for a couple of weeks and see what he could pick up. A few sherbets and some spiffs on the beach of a fine hotel with a new lover would do him a power of good.

Her name was Aphrodite and she had been here for a very long time, but was seriously thinking of floating back across the foam and up to Mount Olympus, leaving all this aggravation and disappointment behind her. Hundreds, maybe even thousands, of years ago, she had landed on the very same beach where Luke was at that moment lying stoned up to the eyeballs, not in Cyprus, as the legend had it, but in this Caribbean paradise. The intention had been for her to spread love and beauty everywhere; she was after all a goddess and this should have been so easy.

The gods had sent her, sea-borne, to her

destination as innocent and naked as a new babe. A scallop shell blown by the Aeolian winds had carried her ashore, voluptuous and prettier than any picture that has ever been painted. To meet her on the beach had been one of her attendants, holding out a finely embroidered cloak to hide her modesty. That first sight of the turquoise sea and white sand had overwhelmed her, for it was almost as breathtakingly lovely as the delights of Olympus and showed so much promise.

Nevertheless, her task had been foiled by the natural aggression and ill-will of the local inhabitants. Of course, she had had her great successes like Lilith and Luke whose love had lasted until death had so cruelly snatched Luke away. On the other side of the coin there was Evie and Ezra, but there had been many, many cases far, far worse than theirs. She had witnessed murders, abuse and deceit and had been surrounded by blood and screams, by guns, knives and poisons, all in the name of her sacred art. She was, however, a patient goddess and would see if she could salvage some good from this particular drama.

Aphrodite, as is the way of goddesses, looked not a day older than when she had first landed on the beach, her skin still like a peach, her auburn hair still shining and gently curling. She gazed down upon Ezra. With his thick, dark hair and still with hardly a wrinkle to his name, except for the occasional line which made him look even more distinguished, he really was an exceptionally good-looking man. Even some of the gods were slightly jealous of his appearance as they looked upon him from above; more so because he didn't have Zeus bullying him and criticising his every move. There were definitely some advantages to being human.

If Aphrodite had not been an immortal and true to her calling, she would like to have claimed him as her own. She couldn't understand Evie's rejection of him. He was a man and therefore should be given a little leeway where matters of the flesh were concerned, but she did believe that both he and Evie should renounce their addiction to some of the plants that grew from the soil. She could very occasionally be quite a prim and proper goddess.

"Oh, Ezra ," she whispered, "I would love to possess you, to feel your arms around me, to feel your kisses upon my skin and, especially, to feel that you would take care of me for ever."

All at once, slumbering Ezra awoke from his drugged dreams. He opened his eyes, trying to focus on the glorious vision before him and his mind geared up into action. This was what he had come to the Caribbean to find. She was totally gorgeous in a green gown accentuating her green cat-like eyes. He saw her suddenly frown at him.

"My name is Aphrodite and you, Ezra, are a bad man. But I'm going to be kind to you and will help you."

Looking Aphrodite up and down, admiring her curvaceous body, he replied, "And I hope, Aphrodite, that you're a bad girl, a very, very bad girl."

Chiding him for his impertinence, she then snapped Evie, sleeping in her distant bed, out of her dreams and summoned her to come to the beach. Aphrodite was working her magic, fulfilling her task of creating love.

"Why the hell am I doing this? What on earth made me decide to do it?" The Caribbean with Ezra was not the place she wanted to be.

From the plane window she could see below her Bermuda, with its fringe of turquoise set in a blue sea which was her favourite place in the whole world. It was the Caribbean, however, that was calling her, as though she were being mentally pushed to follow the route, so Bermuda, that wonderful jewel, would have to wait for another time. Complaining, however, was the last thing she should be doing. Flying first class, was a world away from the yobbos on their cheap flights to Spain, and the hotel that she would be staying in would surely be deluxe. Physically, she was safe and comfortable, but mentally it was another matter. The wild thought had briefly crossed her mind that it was love calling her, but that could not really be so . . . could it? How on earth had she found herself here, because she simply couldn't remember booking her ticket or lugging her wheelie suitcase through the airport?

However, Aphrodite the goddess of love had organised this madness and would not be denied.

For some strange, even magical, reason, once he had set eyes again on Evie all thoughts of Aphrodite went from Luke's mind. She seemed to have been an apparition who just disappeared into thin air, never to be seen or thought of again.

Like Lilith and Luke, their love together was going to be long-lasting, fruitful and eternal. Aphrodite would not now be returning to the foamy sea. She would remain on the earth among mortal folk, fighting for her cause and fulfilling her task as the goddess of love to the best of her ability.

# Inamorata

The cat looked as though he had suffered a severe shock or was perhaps only plain angry, for his tough, raggedy, black fur was standing on end.

He was an intimidating sort of animal.

When Polly first saw him, he was clutched in the crook of his ancient mistress's arm. Mother Bridger was the old crone's name and she ran a very profitable business telling gullible people their fortunes. Her clients were usually working girls, like Polly, who spent their days cleaning and toiling so that other people could have an easy life. Polly received a mere pittance for her labours and so had saved hard for this session to discover what her future had in store for her.

The old woman's cottage was dark and sooty. She would not allow Polly to sit in her presence, for she was mindful of her powers and knew that she was Queen of the Cards – these servant girls did not sit before a queen, for she demanded respect. Her head was covered by a puffy, black hood, but she was not sinister in the slightest degree, for her cheeks were like rosy apples, her eyes twinkled, and she was wearing a clean, faded, floral dress. She looked kind and gentle as though she could easily be someone's grandmother – and probably was.

Indeed, the cat was more daunting than its mistress.

Nevertheless, Polly was worried that she was in the presence of some diabolical force, but when she looked out of the window she saw the reassuring sight of the church spire. Surely the house of God and the house of Evil would not be in such close proximity.

"Well, Polly, there is no need for you ever to be afraid of your future. Whatever happens to you, it will always be to your advantage. You really cannot go wrong."

"But how can this be?"

"Because the cards say so, my dear, and they do not lie. Look at these I have in my hand. The ten of hearts: in other words, a life of happiness, triumph and splendour. The ten of clubs: a sure sign of fortune and success. And, look at this! The eight of clubs which signifies everything a woman's heart could want: a dark man whose affections will bring prosperity. What a lucky girl you are."

"Does that mean that I can do what I want?"

"Of course, you can do anything that comes into your head because you won't change your destiny, for that is set in stone."

Mother Bridger's words were the worst that could possibly have come out of her mouth. At that moment Polly's whole personality changed; she became absolutely fearless and totally daring. Already she had contemplated trying her hand at thieving to improve her lot, and now there was nothing to stop her.

Painted and crimped, Polly made her way into the grand salon decorated with its gilt curlicues, luminous mirrors and lavish furnishings. Whatever the polite, glamorous title that had been assigned to her – courtesan, paramour, concubine – she was really just a plain whore and might as well have been roaming the streets of London plying her trade. The only difference was that now she had a grandiose lifestyle and had changed her name; Polly was the sort of name used only by the lower classes and servants. Her days in service were long over and thus she had become Apollonia, beloved inamorata of many men. In fact, any man who saw her was immediately drawn to her like a bee to a honey pot.

Small, kittenish with a mass of naturally curly hair that had been styled to conform to the latest fashion, today she was awash with precious pearls; around her neck, on her head, hanging from her ears. How she had acquired these was through sleight of hand, for she was an expert at distracting people's attention and stealing away their belongings. She had always been desired and, indeed, abused since she was young, with no one to look after her, no one to love her. She had passed through a hard, heartless upbringing, but today was a day of triumph.

The high-born gentlemen of the gathering were full of admiration; they all recognised beauty when they saw it. The ladies, of course, ignored her and would not acknowledge her presence.

Here she was finally at Heywood Palace where she had always aimed to be. It was not the royal court, but for her it was almost as good.

She sat on a chaise longue and decorously draped herself upon it – a presumption if ever there was one. Lord Frederick Heywood, the duke's heir, thinking what a little hussy she was, sidled up to her and bowed. Everyone was looking and was riveted by the scene. Being a man of the world he had no delusions about her true calling.

"You know what I think, my dear? I think that you are totally delicious, like quince in brandy."

Those who were near enough to hear either gasped or laughed. He was such a wag was Lord Freddie! Polly looked at him, fluttering her eyelashes.

"Why, how kind you are, sir. Though I think I might have preferred to be something sweeter, like a strawberry cream."

"And what is your name, my little strawberry cream?"

"I am Apollonia, sir."

The conversation continued; his compliments becoming so flowery and exaggerated that Polly wanted to giggle. In one way or another she had heard it all before, but from lips rougher and less educated than his. She was a very astute little girl and could see through him as he could see through her. She had no illusions about men and their wiles and he was a typical man: self-centred, his mind focused on his own needs, wanting only to use her as a bed-fellow. The beautiful, white swans who were floating so gracefully on the lake in the grounds of this great house and who were faithful unto death, had more love in one feathered wing than a man had in the whole of his body.

From behind fans, through lorgnettes and

over spectacles the Duke and his guests watched the performance. Women more beautiful than Polly had played the female lead to Freddie's role as a romantic lover and they had all, sooner or later, been cast aside and replaced.

Lying there languishing on the chaise longue, she thought of her present lover, Rupert, a fine man and colonel of the regiment, who had set her up in a splendid town house and had even given her a smart carriage to take her on her shopping expeditions.

Poor Rupert, naturally, had no idea of the height to which her ambition had soared. Old Mother Bridger had assured her that her only direction was upwards and that was just where she was fearlessly headed – the world of the aristocracy was waiting, and Heywood Palace was her first step into it. There was another stately home nearby, but it was owned by a mere earl, not by a Duke.

She had, of course, not been invited to the gathering, but had simply blustered her way in, with lies about a lost invitation card and how the Duke would be so disappointed if she didn't attend. So vivacious and convincing was she that the footman let her enter without a thought. Suddenly she heard a piecing voice assailing her ears.

"Well, we all know what she is, don't we? She should be kept behind closed doors and certainly not allowed to be among people of standing."

The voice belonged to a woman in an over-elaborate, black and white gown with too many frills and furbelows, who bore an uncanny likeness to an eagle, with her long beaked nose and her sharp, beady eyes.

Polly held her temper and kept her thoughts to herself. She looked at the woman and sent a silent message to her.

"You can't imagine how hard I've worked just to be in this room with everyone looking down their noses at me. But one fine day they will pay for their behaviour, for I will remember their scorn. You, Lady High-Hat, in your very tasteless dress, will wish that you had not insulted me, for I shall make it my particular pleasure to oust you from society and into the gutter."

At that precise moment, Polly saw something moving stealthily among people's legs. It was Mother Bridger's strange cat.

As he moved towards her, he gazed into her eyes, winked and then disappeared as though into thin air; she actually watched him fade away in front of her. Had he really been there? Is that what she had truly seen?

It wasn't possible, was it? Anyway, she'd

think about it later, for she had other things to attend to at the moment.

Polly turned over in the great, downy bed and looked at Freddie's sweet face, devoid in sleep of its roguish expression. The sun was shining through a chink in the heavy curtains, so it promised to be a beautiful day in every way: trotting elegantly side-saddle in the park with her riding instructor; lunching al fresco by the lake; tea with the Duke and Duchess, which would be fine if only His Grace would desist from passing his fingers across her décolleté and slyly licking her neck when he had the opportunity.

As it turned out, the day did not continue as promised, for suddenly the sun went behind a cloud and it began to drizzle. Within half-an-hour there were cats and dogs racing at great speed away from the gathering storm clouds. In fact, if you were of an imaginative frame of mind, you would have sworn that you could actually hear the dogs baying and growling in the distance as the thunder drew near.

Unfortunately, as you will see, the day was going to grow much, much worse. Because of the foul weather, there was a change of plan and the riding lesson was replaced by a carriage ride; she and Freddie were ensconced in the comfort and warmth of the carriage, wrapped snugly in rugs, a picnic basket filled with all sorts of delicacies on the seat opposite, which they would eat later.

It was four o'clock in the afternoon. The air sizzled with lightning fire and exploded with thunder as a figure suddenly appeared out of the gloom. As they travelled up the long drive towards the grand portico of the palace, the figure raised its arms and caused the driver and the horses to come to an abrupt halt, throwing Polly and Freddie onto the floor. In fact, they couldn't have moved one inch farther. It was as if they had been turned to stone.

The gloom seemed to disappear from around the figure and it became illuminated by an eerie halo. It was a familiar figure whom Polly immediately recognised, for Mother Bridger was still wearing the same black hood and faded floral dress that she had when last seen.

Her face, however, had been transfigured: aged and wrinkled, washed white and wasted. Her eyes stared so strangely that Polly and Freddie were transfixed. Gone were the rosy cheeks and the twinkling eyes – this was no one's kindly grandmother. She beckoned and the two lovers nervously descended from the carriage. Luckily for them, the rain was having a rest after so much effort. At her skirts stood the cat hissing and spitting out venom.

Suddenly, another figure stole into the limelight in his splendid regimental uniform, sword drawn, grinding his teeth in anger. This was the first time Rupert had seen the Heywood property and, more importantly, Freddie. He had murder in his heart but, being an honourable man, he was not going to leave his opponent weaponless and undefended, so he drew another sword from his scabbard and handed it to Freddie.

"I imagine that you know who I am, sir."

In fact, Freddie had not the slightest idea. Naturally enough, Polly had never spoken of him.

"I am afraid, sir, that you have the advantage of me. But I should be grateful to know the cause of something that could possibly harm me." The reason was made clear and clearest of all was that Rupert loved Polly, Polly loved Freddie and Freddie loved only himself. The old crone stood smiling before them.

"Well, Polly," she croaked, "let's see how this little problem resolves itself, shall we? Right, gentleman, you may begin."

There was nothing she enjoyed more than a bit of drama and she knew she was in for a treat.

She had no idea who the winner would be for she was a fraud and could no more read the cards or foretell the future than fly in the air. In fact, that is not completely true because she could indeed fly in the air and she did possess some very frightening and potent powers, but clairvoyance was not one of them. It was always amusing to see what happened to those credulous wide-eyed girls as they so trustingly watched her reading the cards. The cut and thrust of the duel lasted some time, but there was no clear winner for both men were seriously wounded. Rupert died first, in the damp evening air with no one to help him, except an ineffectual Polly. Mother Bridger rubbed her hands together in pleasure.

Freddie was carried home in the carriage and for two days was tended and nursed with the utmost care and attention, but he was doomed, and died in the Duchess's arms. Mother Bridger too watched his end because she enjoyed a good finale to a story but, having made herself invisible, no one knew she was there. The cat also thought what a splendid scene this was, purring silently with satisfaction.

The King came to Freddie's funeral.

The estate workers lined the drive as he

passed by in his grand carriage pulled by the most beautiful horses imaginable. Among those watching was Polly who had always known that one day she would mix with royalty, but not in this way. She had been duped by a wicked old crone, and her self-confidence had started to wane.

The Duchess had thrown her out of the house and confiscated her beautiful dresses and jewellery. If Polly had not entered their lives Freddie would still be alive.

Polly so hoped, when the cortège passed by, that some rich gentleman would notice her standing there in the one pretty dress left to her. The only person to take any note of her, however, was the eagle-like woman to whom she had given the name Lady High-hat and whom she'd sworn to send to the gutter. The proud woman looked her up and down from behind her black veil and then tossed her head and looked away.

It was now Polly who was in the gutter, but as she stood in tears, bewailing her sad plight, she watched Mother Bridger's cat striding purposefully in her direction. His fur was standing on end as he rubbed himself against her ankles. He meowed loudly, sat at her feet and, winking, looked up at her. His face bore a defiant look and she knew she was stuck with him.

So off they both went together. Polly knew she had to start again from scratch, but she had gained much knowledge and wisdom on the way. Therefore, she looked around for something that she could pilfer because, like her cat, she was defiant and decided she would not allow life to get the better of her. Especially, she would not forget Lady High-Hat, but that's another tale.

# Strange Trick of Light

The light was fading over Venice and the last remains of the day's sun could be seen disappearing around the curve of a narrow canal. It was a red glow that reflected on the water like blood.

At the end of the narrow pavement, which ran along the little houses fronting the water, was a wide flight of steps – to the right another led down to the canal where a lone gondolier stood, a cigarette in his hand, as his boat gently rocked against the bottom step.

Staggering on the upward flight, Alessandra was going towards her apartment, its snug, stone balcony full of vibrantly coloured flowers. She had removed her high-heeled shoes to save herself from a broken ankle and to aid her progress. She was drunk, with just about enough breath and strength to reach her front door, outside which she flopped down upon the step, unable to find the energy to turn the key in the lock. Her heart was beating ominously in her chest and she felt sick. She promised herself that never again would she ever touch the demon drink, but then she said that nearly every evening.

Once the door was open, she crawled on her hands and feet into her elegant, little sitting room and reached up to a side-table to turn on the light. Thus, like a stage show, she was suddenly illuminated allowing her audience to watch all the action. She was never to know this, for the two old ladies in the house opposite whose entertainment she was, were usually hidden in the dark. They did not want her to realise the pleasure she gave them. They had a television, but much preferred the live action she afforded them in no small measure. Even their large, white cat seemed enthralled by it all and his tail waved furiously in anticipation.

Each evening the three of them watched the latest episode of Alessandra's life. She was usually inebriated and tottering as she made her way home, but not always alone for she seemed to have an endless supply of men friends which was really what they preferred – much more interesting viewing!

However, a solo performance also had its charms. Tonight, they decided to peep through the slats of their shutters just to put her off the scent in case she had sussed out something of their spying. This annoyed the cat no end for he felt left out, not being able to see properly what was happening. Why couldn't they all have a clearer view – it was so much easier? He liked to be able to look down at the gondolier who had been relaxing here for the last few evenings. Added to which cats – well, at least this cat – had an appreciation of beauty and enjoyed watching the changing shadows on the building walls and the reflections in the canal as dusk approached, especially the peculiar red tinge of water which surrounded the gondola as though some artist had painted it there on purpose.

They actually did feel uncomfortable about what they were doing – after all, it was spying on someone's private life, wasn't it? Moreover, they had literally turned the cat into a peeping Tom! They wouldn't give it up, however, for it was too much fun – and, anyway, they had no other hobbies, except for very basic cooking and doing the odd bit of shopping. Embroidery, crocheting, painting, nothing of that sort interested them. As for computing, well, that was an alien world and they were completely unwilling to have anything to do with tweeting or twittering or whatever it was people did on those awful machines. They were just two nosey old dears, with a cat in tow, who would spend much of their waking hours speculating and discussing what they had witnessed the evening before.

If, however, they had watched their ancient television set they could have learned an awful lot more about their neighbour because she was something of a celebrity – a girl who predicted for the Italian nation what was in store for them weather-wise. The staid military meteorologists of yore had had their day. Like all the weather girls, she was extremely attractive – the usual style – long, dark hair, a good dollop of eye make-up and lots of leg on show to keep the Italian male libido satisfied. Her men friends adored her, because not only was she beautiful but also, as she had made it on the small screen, perhaps she could put in a good word for them career-wise.

Her audience watched as she sat consuming virtually a whole pot of coffee to try to sober herself up. She really must stop all this drinking, for only that morning she had noticed a few lines appearing at the sides of her eyes – crow's feet at her age – surely not. "You silly bitch," she muttered to herself. "You've really let yourself go! And what about my liver – can't be doing it much good, can I?" Heaven only knows what her mother would think to see her in such a state.

The remainder of the evening made dull viewing for her hidden audience, until she suddenly opened the French windows onto her balcony and stepped outside to get some fresh air. She was smoking a cigarette; another habit she'd have to cut back on. It was such a beautiful evening and, looking down, she saw the gondolier also having a smoke. He's rather good looking she thought and standing on tiptoes she looked down upon him. He'd heard her doors opening and gazing up at her, waved his hand. She hadn't really taken much notice of him on his previous evenings there, but for some reason at that very instant, he suddenly appeared terribly appealing – probably because tonight she was man-less!

Her audience, meanwhile, let their curiosity get the better of them and, careful to keep in the shadows, actually went so far as to open the shutters. Having the best seats in the house they couldn't possibly miss this piece of theatre – for Alessandra very rarely went onto her balcony, mostly just leaving the French doors open. The cat was quite overcome with excitement and started meowing, so they gave him a piece of chicken to keep him quiet.

They listened intently to the exchange between the weather-girl and the gondolier. His face was partly hidden by his woven straw hat with its red-coloured ribbon on the brim and around the crown, but even so you could tell that he had an appealing personality that would have attracted anyone. His deep voice carried across the canal water, up to the secret watchers opposite and up the wide steps leading to Alessandra's flat: everyone hearing him loud and clear.

"Why don't you come down here, signorina? I could take you for a little ride in my gondola, if you so wished."

"Far better that you should come up here, signor," she answered, thinking that she really didn't have the strength to totter all the way down the steps in her rather fragile state.

"Go on, signorina!" thought the cat. "Please come down to the water's edge!" He so much wanted to see them move together towards the little bridge near the curve where the canal disappeared from sight.

The gondolier smiled for he didn't really care which way the conversation went for it would all finish as it was intended. He made sure that his boat was tied firmly to the mooring pole with its red and white spiral stripes and jumped onto dry land, striding confidently up the wide steps to Alessandra's small apartment.

The hidden audience watched in fascination,

for the beautifully ornate, metal lamps on the walls of the nearby houses suddenly lit up and their view was thus perfect for whatever happened inside or out.

From their sideboard, out came a packet of toffee-covered popcorn and the evening glass of prosecco was poured carefully into two crystal glasses as the old ladies settled down for the performance. What a naughty pair they were! What prurient minds they had! Sharing the popcorn, the white cat sat in his usual place on the top of the sofa behind their heads, sensing the excitement, but also with a sensation that he couldn't quite put his paw on. They watched Alessandra showing the gondolier into her sitting room and before long the prospective lovers were drinking and laughing.

She had completely forgotten her resolution to lead a non-alcoholic existence and he was having such weird, black thoughts about her and about the world at large, that the old dears could never possibly have imagined them.

She just wished that he would remove his hat – it was so impolite for a gentleman to sit like that. She would like to have had a closer view of him, but his face, rather insubstantial, seemed to be moving in and out of sight, not surprising considering the amount she'd had to drink

"What is your name?" Alessandra had asked the gondolier, but he wouldn't tell her.

"It's a puzzle and I won't tell you just quite yet. But you will learn it very soon, I promise!"

"What a silly boy you are! What is so special about your name that you can't tell me?"

Unfortunately for her, she would not have long to wait for the answer.

The conversation, as was only to be expected, gradually became more and more suggestive and raunchy because, of course, it was alcohol-fuelled lust that had made her invite him into her web, like a black widow spider, ready to poison her mate. She had invited so many young men into her snare; never, of course, to kill them, but merely to have use of their bodies for her own gratification, as her neighbours had so enjoyed witnessing. She did, however, have that niggling desire to learn his name, so started to quiz him. "Francesco? Lorenzo? Gabriele? Come on, please tell me!" Each suggestion was answered with a shake of his head.

"Matteo? Marcello?"

His dark eyes bored into hers.

"You're getting warmer. You're nearly there. Yes, my name does begin with an M. Keep going!"

By this time, she felt quite cross and upset, determined to get the right answer, but each attempt only ended in disappointment.

"Martelli? Mariano? Michelangelo?

"Wrong, wrong, wrong. Alright, I'll tell you." He stood up, went towards her and whispered his secret into her ear. "It's Morte, Alessandra, Morte! It's Death!"

She gazed through a mist at his skull, from which all the skin had disappeared into thin air, she gazed at his skinless, bony hands which had at last politely removed his gondolier's hat, so that she could see him in all his horror.

Suddenly her heart started to beat and pulsate at great speed and black shadows began to dart in front of her eyes. The gondolier was telling the truth. He had come for her. He was Death. He'd been waiting for days on the canal for just this moment.

Thus the old dears watched the final episode of the series, but the finale was so horrific that never again would they ever spy on anyone. In fact, they were so terrified, catching a glimpse of Death, that it was a miracle that he didn't have to enter their apartment and carry them down the back stairs and round to the canal where the funereal black gondola awaited Alessandra. She didn't, however, go alone, on her journey to the cemetery island of San Michele, for Death had another victim to accompany her, an unexpected one. The poor, white cat, overcome with panic, gave an almighty leap from the back of the sofa onto the window sill, crashed through the glass and was hurled into the air, only to find himself impaled on a sharp, gilt ornamental statue at the front of the gondola. His blood streamed into the water to merge with the red reflection that had surrounded the gondola since Death's arrival.

Drops of rain suddenly started to fall as though the skies had opened up with tears to mourn the weather-girl. The last view the weeping old ladies had of their beloved cat was as the gondola drifted through the moonless, rainy night, under the small bridge and then round the curve to be lost forever from view.

# The Changing Sea

"Why don't you listen to the sea, Jethro? It's such a lovely sound; the gurgling, the rushing! It is enchanting! Just turn your ipod off, just for a moment, just for me! Please!"

"Don't be so foolish! It's only water and, heaven knows, it's cost me enough just to sit here beside it, without wanting to listen to it! Believe me; Caribbean water is no different from Dover Beach water, except that it's a hell of a lot more expensive!"

"Jethro, can't you see the little, white horses riding on the sparkling, blue waves! It's gorgeous! Just put your book down and look!"

"It's surf, for God's sake! Surf!"

"I know it's surf but see how the sun shines upon it. Just think of all the galleons that must lie wrecked in the depth of the ocean. Mermaids and pirates and coral!"

"What on Earth's got into you – a touch of the sun, is it? Turned poetic all of a sudden, have you? From the sort of rubbish you read I'm surprised that your closed little mind could possibly extend beyond the world of Posh and Becks, let alone drift off into the ocean!"

"But Jethro, Posh and Becks come here! They like the Caribbean! Everyone likes it."

"Except me, Dolly, except me! The heat, the sand, the sheer boredom of it all and all these phonies with their expensive watches, talking about their Bentleys and their Mercedes. Worst of all Dolly, you, – having to endure your inane conversation day in day out!"

"Oh, Jethro, how could you say that, how could you? I think that must be the cruellest thing you've ever said to me! This is supposed to be our dream holiday, a once in a lifetime experience, our togetherness time."

"Our togetherness time! Where did you pick that one up from? You really should give up reading that mushy rubbish!"

It's surprisingly easy to run out of love and sometimes, suddenly, it simply hurtles away of its own accord, out of the blue with no warning. As it did for Dolly, lying there on the beach that beautiful morning under a tropical sky!

What a long way to come to discover that the man she had thought she loved until a moment ago didn't actually like her very much and that she had been sharing her life and her bed with a stranger.

Smug and self righteous was how she now saw him. Always putting her down! Always imposing his will upon hers! The only reason they were here, which was where she had often begged to come, was because Mr Collins, chairman of the board, had recommended it! Why had she not seen it before – his petty jealousies, his unwillingness to enjoy new experiences, his lack of imagination! His sheer nastiness!

Whatever he said to her now wouldn't matter, really wouldn't hurt her, because she had suddenly discovered a secret place in her mind, a place where he could never find her, never follow her. A beautiful place of refuge, where she could completely erase him from her thoughts! Yes, under the sea – that is where she would let her imagination wander freely.

What did Jethro really think of her? Well, she'd have been extremely surprised if she could have looked into his heart as he lay there beside her in his bright, red Bermuda shorts, his fat, little body covered in so much sun screen that he would return to England as white as when he boarded the plane at Heathrow. Because the answer was that he loved her, loved her desperately, and needed her desperately. He just wished that she wasn't so damned thick! Was she perhaps losing her marbles, he wondered, with all this talk of pirates and Spanish galleons! No, she would be fine! Nothing that another three weeks on this beach wouldn't sort out! My God, he thought, three weeks – if only it weren't all so tedious! What he wouldn't give to be trout fishing in Scotland!

"It's the music of the sea, Jethro" she said. "Music pure and simple, just as much as the symphonies you like to listen to. There's nothing ugly and jarring about the music that the sea makes – not like some of the things you like! Can't you see what I mean?"

Of course, he couldn't see! How could he?

"Shut up about it, Dolly. For God's sake, put a spoke in it, can't you?"

So off she floated into her own little world and luxuriated in it, while she filled it with exotic sea life – with beautiful whales who called plaintively to each other, with mermaids who drew combs of coral through their long wavy tresses, with rotting galleons from whose masts there still hung tattered sails and pennants! The anemones and the underwater flowers that shimmered as the sunlight penetrated the surface of the sea – how wondrous they were! All the new friends that she would make! Valiant sea captains, princesses kidnapped from their castles by swashbuckling, blacked-bearded Barbary pirates, dolphins on whose backs she would ride, holding tightly onto their scarlet, silken reins.

Suddenly, Dolly decided to wander across the white sand to the edge of the sea! How wonderful it was to feel the warmth of the water around her ankles, to see the palm trees silhouetted against the amazingly blue sky!

"Bit late to think about learning to swim now, isn't it, Dolly? Anyway, I would have thought that there are already enough whales in the sea without you joining them!"

She bit her lips and gulped back a sob at this unkindness, and Jethro bit his lips and wondered why on earth he had said it, but he couldn't say sorry, could he? It simply wasn't his way! Anyway, Dolly by this time had made her escape and was once again planning her new home! Having designed a little scalloped-edged grotto in which to live, its entrance illuminated by a beam of sunlight, she was now busily decorating it with gossamer curtains woven by sea spiders and furnishing it with gilt tables and beautifully embroidered chairs that the mermen had carried for her from a sunken ship. On the grotto wall was an oval mirror adorned with the pearls that she'd carefully plucked from oyster shells.

"Are you going to hang about all day sloshing in the water or are we going up to the restaurant to have some lunch! I'm hungry!"

So, Dolly reluctantly dragged herself back to reality and quickly wrapped herself in the emerald green sarong that she'd bought from John Lewis's only a few days ago. Up the beach they trudged, this ordinary-looking, middle-aged couple. No one watching them would have imagined the sea change that had taken place in their relationship – Dolly, now resentful and withdrawn; Jethro, now sensing that in some strange fashion his world was out of kilter and would remain so.

Lunch on the terrace overlooking the ocean, was a tense affair fraught with a potential landmine of faux pas and misunderstandings. The menu, of course, was mainly composed of seafood. So while Jethro sat there hungrily tucking in to prawns and calamari and a nice plump piece of red snapper, Dolly picked at her salad, trying not to think of the pain that the poor prawns and the poor calamari and the poor red snapper had endured in order to arrive on Jethro's plate. Suddenly, she put down her knife and fork and said desperately:

"I'm sorry, Jethro, but I feel as though I've a migraine coming on – I think I'll just go and lie down in the dark."

"Don't be silly, Dolly, you don't have migraines, so just sit here with me and have another glass of wine. I don't know what's got into you today – not going all dramatic on me, are you? Not another touch of the Posh and Becks, is it?"

Dolly cringed inwardly and tried to think of her beautiful grotto under the sea, so peaceful, so friendly – no enemies, no confrontations! More beautiful than anything else there, were her favourites, the baby octopuses. Dolly loved octopuses – so intelligent, such good parents to their offspring. Dolly and Jethro had never had children, mainly because Jethro had felt it irresponsible when the world was already so overpopulated. Dolly, however, was going to make up for this terrible void in her life, for under the ocean there would be a nursery, not just for octopuses, but for babies of all kinds – the crabs, the sea horses, the sea snails, the balloon fish, the damselfish – she would care for them all. For there was certainly no one here on land to whom she could now give her love!

The rest of the afternoon they spent on their terrace overlooking the hotel swimming pool, slumbering and reading, reading and slumbering, but certainly not talking, for there was absolutely nothing to say.

Gradually the sun disappeared below the horizon and the sky produced its usual palette of amazing colours. Then, suddenly, the moon was shining down, telling them that it was time to dress for dinner. Oh God, thought Jethro, three more weeks of having to cram his considerable flesh into a penguin suit – already he'd put on weight!

Dolly had gone in before him to start to get ready – tonight was to be the first outing for the bright blue evening dress that she'd purchased online from Marks and Spencer, or rather that he'd ordered for her, Dolly, of course, being totally computer illiterate. Poor Dolly, not always too clever at choosing the right clothes either, but she'd pass muster. Also, she had liked the dress which was the important thing he supposed.

Jethro lay on the bed waiting for Dolly to come out of the bathroom so that he could have his shower. He waited… and waited! Why did it always take her so long to do things?

"For heaven's sake, woman, get a bloody move on, will you!"

When there was no reply he got up and opened the bathroom door. No Dolly! Only her evening bag on the vanity unit. Where the hell was she?

Well, if he'd been walking along the moonlit beach at that moment he would have had the answer to his question, for the blue evening dress was lying crumpled on the sand and Dolly, her white naked body like marble under the cold, silver moon, was stepping into the ocean, walking farther and farther out to sea until her feet lost contact with the land. She was so happy, for she was going home – to her grotto, to her friends, to her babies. She would perhaps, however, have been less happy, and much amazed, if she'd been able to hear the sobs, see the tears that Jethro shed for her later that evening, as he stood on the beach with the police, her blue dress clasped in his trembling hands.

"I love you, Dolly!" he whispered. "I love you!"

"But it's too late, Jethro, isn't it?" She would have answered, "Much too late for us now!".

# The Enemy

She broke into a smile. "I'll get you next time!" she said. Power, exhilaration; this what she demanded from her meetings with him. He was a cute, little fellow, his fur shining like burnished gold under the sun, but he was the enemy and she was out to get him. Today he'd won, but her moment of triumph was undoubtedly on its way. Nevertheless, her victory would be tinged with sadness.

Victoria sat there watching him disappear into the distance – both she and her horse were tired, so heaven only knew how tired the fox must feel, especially as he was no youngster. It seemed as if they had been having this same confrontation for years. She found herself actually raising her hand in farewell to him, as he vanished into the woodland.

Following the rest of the hunt, she set a steady pace back to the village, the movement of the horse's steaming body between her legs providing an almost sensual satisfaction. By the time they arrived back at the pub from which they had started, the usual mixture of hunt saboteurs and those who almost lived for the sport were mingled together. What sort of people were these townies with their silly, sentimental ideas? Obviously the same sort of peasantry who failed to recognise the magnificence and pageantry of the great battle between bull and matador – yes, the great unwashed, completely unmindful and ignorant of country ways and traditions, living in their small semis and terraced houses.

Victoria would never, ever forget the pride that she had experienced when her face had been blooded at the first kill that she had witnessed. She must only have been about twelve years old at the time, almost sixty years ago, but it was a memory that would remain with her always. She looked down at her old, claw-like hands and knew that she would never forgo the great pleasure that hunting gave her, that she would sit high in the saddle until the day she died: listening to the baying of the hounds, the pounding of the hooves beneath her, the echoing of the magical horn in the air around her. She supposed that, one day, she might even forget what she was chasing – but she would be there!

Another bone of the same contention was being was being chewed over in front of the pub under a willow tree where Julian and Mark were sitting, pints in hand, both their T-shirts adorned with a badger's face under which was emblazoned the words 'not guilty'.

"It seems that anything that is beautiful they have to destroy it; whether it be deer, or badger or fox."

Victoria, still on her horse looked down imperiously upon them with a gin and tonic in her hand.

"Of course, they are beautiful: we all know that. But how would you feel if you were a farmer and saw your livelihood decimated by the disease and the slaughter that these creatures bring?"

"It's your attitude of superiority, Victoria, the pleasure that you obviously get from killing that especially disgusts me. Some of your hunting pals can barely string two words together but put them on a horse and they think of themselves as gods. They don't give a damn about the countryside and the traditions you all talk about. It's just blood lust: going after something that can't defend itself."

Victoria looked around at some of her fellow huntsmen and secretly thought to herself that in some cases this was not too far from the truth.

These days the parvenus with their nouveau riche money could get anything and everything. The old families who should be here, as they had been for generations, could no longer afford such luxuries as horses and hounds. School fees and the upkeep of crumbling houses took all their resources. Julian and Mark, for example, came from just such a background; their parents must have been overwhelmingly disappointed to have produced offspring with such silly ideas.

Fenella was an exceptionally beautiful young woman, thought Mark and Julian: she sat so magnificently on her horse that, whenever they saw her looking like this, they could sense a slight shimmer of the glamour that surrounded the hunting fraternity. Victoria knew that they had lost interest in what she was saying, so left them to their salacious thoughts. Yes, she thought, undeniably Fenella was lovely; from a good family, her father managing director of a large engineering works. She had been a member of the hunt for only a short time but was already impeccable in her adherence to the strict behaviour code of foxhunting and to its dress etiquette. Victoria hoped that it would all come to mean as much to Fenella as it had to her… but poor Victoria, deceived by what she wanted to believe, betrayed by appearances, had totally misunderstood; Fenella was out to get her.

As Victoria went for her evening walk across the fields the sun was going down; it was a perfect setting at the end of a perfect day. She was thinking of her foxy enemy and wondering where he lived. Was he in the wood, hiding himself in a deserted burrow or perhaps snuggled up amid the dense undergrowth? She was confident that she would easily recognise him, for she often saw him in her dreams at night and was half in love with him. After all, other people loved their dogs and cats, often to distraction, so why should she not love this wonderful fox? Their lives were intertwined in some magical fashion that she could not explain.

Feeling tired from the day's exertions and perhaps unwise to have walked so far, Victoria decided that she would go through the wooden fence that separated the fields from the wood and sit on a tree stump to rest her weary legs, before starting the long trek home. She sat there in the gloom not moving, hardly daring to breathe, for she had heard a faint rustling sound in the bushes. Suddenly, out of the corner of her eye, she saw a moving shadow and, slowing turning her head, there he was: her lover and her enemy. At almost the same moment, he realised that she was there and he, too, turned his head towards her. For a split-second their eyes met and then he went quickly on his way.

Victoria could not let him go so easily and stood up intending to follow him if it were at all possible. All at once, she felt an excruciating pain in her ankle and found herself trapped in a badgers' drag snare, her feet tangled in the wire, but the more she struggled the tighter grew her bonds, her old bones inexorably shackled. She cried out for help, but there was nothing and no one to aid her. The only sound was that of the fox barking in the distance; he certainly would not approach her or relieve her suffering, even if able to do so by some quirk of magic.

She must then have lost consciousness for the next thing that registered in her mind was talking and laughter; voices that she recognised: Julian, Mark and Fenella. Thank God she was safe! Everything was going to be alright.

"Well, well, look who we have here!" said Mark, "You've certainly had a busy day, haven't you, Victoria? I think I would call your present predicament 'reaping your just reward' – of course, in the most ironical of senses!"

"So now," added Julian's voice, "you know how it feels, Victoria, to be helplessly trapped and to have your limbs mangled for sheer sport."

Victoria tried in vain to speak, but she was too shocked, too frail to utter a word. A pitiful, moaning cry was the only sound she could make.

"No one's property is safe from you, Victoria. Your damned hunt came into our garden and killed my darling dog, Dolly. I swore that, by one means or another I would have my revenge, and here it is without my having to lift a finger!" laughed Fenella, shining a powerful torch into the stricken woman's eyes, blinding her for several seconds. "You know all about lamping, don't you, Victoria? The lamper can see the reflection of the animal's eyes and either sets his dogs on to it or straightaway shoots it." Then, in a gesture of sheer viciousness, she directed the harsh light again towards her captured prey.

Mark looked at his watch. "I'm afraid we have to leave you now – we just have enough time to fit in a few more beers before the pub closes… And by the way, Victoria, I don't advise you to try escaping by gnawing off your foot like some of your victims. You have neither the time nor the strength left to do it."

"One of us comes here most evenings to inspect the traps and snares so that we can rescue the animals that have been caught. Unfortunately, in your case, there will be no salvation and you will be left to your own devices." Julian smiled at the withered, terrified face as though he were trying to charm her. "So, we shall wish you a fond farewell … and, of course, a lingering death." He bowed elegantly and, as he turned away, blew her a kiss.

Julian, Mark and Fenella then walked off slowly into the gloom, leaving the old woman to her fate, her cries becoming fainter and fainter. Nevertheless, they did not emerge untouched from their encounter in the wood, for, whenever a fox barked in the stillness of the night, all three were destined to wonder at their own cruelty. Henceforth, they kept well away from the sight of any hunt, for they knew in their hearts that they had descended to the same level as the foxhunters and the badger-baiters.

# The Lord of Death

Suddenly everyone in that most beauteous of temples, the one dedicated to the great God Osiris, turned and stared. Although they were all priests and should have known better, they stared, stared intrusively, impolitely, absolutely fascinated; they stared while the sacred incense filled the air with the ravishing scent of sandalwood. Of course, no one saw it rising, swirling, carrying their prayers and devotions up to the green-faced God who ruled over the Land of the Dead, for all eyes were directed at the Queen as she stood with her back against one of the towering pillars, screaming and screaming and screaming, her open mouth seeming to fill her whole face.

This was a complete transformation from loveliness into ugliness; wrinkles had appeared where they had not been before; her gaping mouth, where several teeth were missing, revealed her fondness for sweetmeats, sugared almonds and candied fruits. A torrent of tears sprang from her eyes and even dripped onto the cold, stone floor of the temple, leaving little wet patches where they had fallen, tears not of sorrow, but of sheer, naked fury. In her hand she held a beautiful, gold-handled dagger and suddenly with a smooth, sinewy action she lunged forward and stabbed it into the neck of the poor, hapless messenger who was kneeling in front of her. Again, and again she found her target and made sure that there could only be one outcome – such a suitable ending in that place dedicated to Death.

Those watching drew back in horror at the ferocity of the action. From whence and for what reason had come such emotion, such cruelty? Thrown onto the ground there lay the crumpled, blood-smeared message; until the Queen, like a spoilt child thwarted in its desires, furiously ground the papyrus into shreds with her foot.

Everything was gradually being stripped away. Julius Caesar dead! Mark Antony dead! Her lovers both! She had seduced them both, she had seduced Rome itself. In fact, never had there been a man who had not been seduced by her charms – or almost never. Until now! Because, of course, Octavian had never wanted her and now it was he who was coming for her – to make her his prisoner and to parade her through the streets of

Alexandria like some little slave girl. Or so the message had informed her.

By this time the Queen had stopped screaming and had slid down the pillar so that she was now slumped against it, her arms hanging down lifelessly and her plump hands resting palms up on the stone floor. Kneeling on either side of her, Charmian and Iras, her handmaidens, wafted feathery, turquoise fans in front of her ashen face, hoping to revive her.

Away from the coolness of the interior of the temple, the heat outside was blisteringly hot, overwhelming so, the air still. Flies moved about lethargically, settling every so often on the faces of those waiting for the Emperor Octavian to claim his victim. Cleopatra was their Queen and they loved her for she cared for her people, had made Egypt great, and most endearingly of all, she had learned to speak Egyptian – no other member of her family had ever bothered to do that before!

Nevertheless, they were anxious to see the grand spectacle, witness the great drama that would no doubt unfold in front of their eyes. After all it was only human nature to want to do so. In the distance they could hear the sound of the approaching trumpets and drums and suddenly through the heat haze marched into view the warriors of Rome with their javelins, spears and shields, accompanied by small, lumbering African elephants, which they had obviously acquired en route.


When the great, ornate doors were suddenly flung open the torches of the temple flickered as the air stirred and Octavian's voice rang out.

"Sorceress! Witch! Bitch! I've come to get you!"

His eyes almost passed over her as she lay on the floor, but when he looked down at the little tableau at his feet, he was immediately struck by how vulnerable, how powerless the great Pharaoh now seemed. His heart almost missed a beat. What did that signify he fleetingly wondered!

Charmian and Iras lifted their dark eyes to his face and he could sense their fear, see the slight trembling of their limbs. Their mistress stirred, moaned and then allowed herself to be lifted up so that now she stood, unsteadily, face to face with the Roman Emperor. He looked into her eyes, which resembled deep pools of violet and he could see the anger in their depths. "So, the day of reckoning has finally arrived, hasn't it? Your people will at last see you as you really are – a small, ordinary woman, unremarkable when all the paint and powder have been wiped from your face, nothing special for the eye once the fine clothes and rich jewels have been removed. A long, tiring walk through the city in the noonday sun will soon cut you down to size!

On her forehead, attached to a gorgeously decorated head band, the Queen wore the golden uraeus, the sacred, rearing cobra that represented royalty and fire – and, most especially, eternal life. It glinted and sparkled as she met Octavian's gaze and he was forced to look away, almost blinded by its radiance and by the hatred that flashed from her violet eyes. He started walking up and down in front of her, pushing the priests roughly aside as he did so, declaiming his victory, asserting his dominance over her. However, Cleopatra had not been present on the battlefield, had not sailed the seas at the head of her fleet for nothing and, now, recovered from learning the dreadful fate for which she was destined at Octavian's hands, she knew without any doubt what she must do.

"You defile this temple with your presence – this holy place is for me only and for my priests – no ordinary mortal is allowed in here."

"And your handmaidens…?"

"They have special dispensation – they are loved by their Queen and never leave her side, even here!"

She clenched her fists by her side, lifted her head proudly and held him in her gaze. He felt hypnotised as he listened to her deep, sultry voice and found himself, against his will, forced to look into her eyes. She really was a sorceress, an enchantress for here she was weaving her spell over him, and he could not help but imagine how things might have been between them if he had not been so intent on mastering the world.

"I ask you, Octavian, to remember that no man is truly great unless he shows some mercy to his victims – especially to one as innocent as I. Let me prepare myself for the humiliation that awaits me. Let me go into the ante-chamber with my handmaidens so that I may take the sacred snake from my forehead and dress myself in clothes more fitting to the slave I'm about to become."

Octavian was not deceived by her words for he knew her to be cunning and shrewd and would not allow her to leave his presence without some assurance that she would not try to escape. So he sent a servant to watch over her and thus the Queen with her handmaidens – and the servant – left Octavian cooling his heels in the great hall of the temple.

However, as soon as the door closed behind them, the handmaidens, seeming to move as one and without giving the unfortunate servant time to collect his thoughts, placed a golden cord around his neck and ended his life in mid breath. Then Iras ran out to the sacred lake, that place of ritual cleansing, and from beneath one of the surrounding palm trees collected a small wicker basket and returned to her mistress.

The Queen, still wearing the sumptuous rearing cobra on her forehead, opened the basket and another cobra, this one made of flesh and blood, reared up to meet her. She smiled and gave a laugh of triumph as it pierced her arm with its fangs and she sank slowly, with infinite grace, down onto the ornately decorated couch that stood on a tiger skin rug.

"I shall have eternal life," she gasped as the venom spread through her body. "I shall be slave to no one. I shall again be with Caesar, with Mark Antony. I shall be Isis; and Osiris, the Lord of Death, will judge my soul favourably."

When Octavian eventually opened the door of the antechamber, he gave a great roar of anger at the scene that met his eyes. The dead Queen lay magnificently arrayed in all her finery on her couch and at the foot of the couch was a basket of figs, figs dipped in hemlock, which had enabled her faithful handmaidens to follow her into the Underworld. Iras lay sprawled on the carpet, her hand still clasping that of her mistress, while Charmian had fallen across the Queen's body.

The priests of Osiris wept and wailed for their dead Pharaoh, while, outside the temple, arose a collective groan from those waiting in the baking heat. Octavian knew in his heart that he had lost something irretrievable, precious, but could not, at that precise moment, quite put into thoughts what that might be.

The cobra, meanwhile, the instrument of her death who had opened for her the door to everlasting happiness, slithered away into a corner and hid in the shadows of the antechamber.

# The Mausoleum

This graveyard was her little kingdom and all these dead people were her subjects. As befits a Queen, she lived in a fine castle; in other words, the finest mausoleum to be found in this stretch of hallowed ground. The spirits of the dead Victorian tycoon and his family with whom she shared her accommodation had, after the first few hours of resistant muttering and moaning, made her feel surprisingly at home. It was four years ago almost to the day that she had first sought shelter with them. The snow had been falling steadily and she had known that she would not survive long without a place of refuge, but fate lent a hand when suddenly she saw a rat scuttle into the mausoleum's slightly ajar entrance.

So here she was, all these years later with her sleeping bag, her gas fire, her thermos, her candles, her radio, her simple cooking utensils and even with her recipe books. Plenty of cushions were dotted around, of course, because they added colour and cosiness to the rather drab décor of her home. A tin of pine-scented Airwick was an absolute necessity to remove the smell of decay – not of the dead Victorians who had long ago decomposed, but of the dead rats and mice that she sometimes found at the back of the mausoleum.

It was a good life – peaceful, solitary, which is how she liked it. Naturally, her neighbours caused her no problems – there was no noise, no quarrels and no boundary disputes. She knew all their names and had found out as much as she could about them from church records and from the other usual sources – the local library, for example, was a fount of information. Her immediate neighbour was Eliza Bentham born 1614, died 1635 – such a short life, but one which Eliza now shared with her husband Peter, died 1640 and her son Jethro, both of whom now lay peacefully on either side of her. Millie's favourite, however, and her best friend, was Nathaniel Porter, born 1802, died 1860. He must have been a good sort – a humble agricultural worker and yet his grave was fit for a prince, decorated with swirling patterns, with curling snakes, with twining vine leaves all lovingly carved into the stone.

Millie made the rounds of her kingdom every

day, even when it poured with rain: she didn't want any of them to feel neglected, unloved by their Queen. She had taken on the responsibility of caring for them – that's what Queens are supposed to do, isn't it? There was always time to have a little chat with them, to pull out a few weeds from around them, sometimes even to sprinkle a few wildflowers over them! Every year, on All Souls' Day, she would buy half a dozen loaves of bread, tubs of butter and make sandwiches filled with delicious strawberry jam. She would then conscientiously visit all her subjects in turn, placing a paper plate of sandwiches on each tomb and beside each plate she would place a paper cup full of lemon squash. She really had no idea who was supposed to look after the graveyard and its inhabitants – presumably the council, but she'd never actually seen a gardener around, which suited her down to the ground. The less chance the better, of being discovered in her cosy, rent-free abode.

The only visitor to the graveyard that she knew of was Bunty – poor old Bunty, poor old girl. Think of any televised portrayal of "a bag lady" and you have a perfect picture of Bunty. Millie suspected that Bunty's situation was as precarious as her own, for she was always rather vague about where and how she lived. However,

Millie was not about to offer her shelter in the mausoleum, even on the most inhospitable of days. She valued her privacy too much for that and, anyway, it could well be that the Victorian tycoon might take offence and she certainly didn't want to stir up twitterings and whistlings of ghostly disapproval, nor indeed to see her cushions being thrown around in a spiritual tantrum.

Millie was only forty-one years but had suffered a hard life. Abandoned by her parents, by numerous foster parents, by her so-called friends, by two fiancés and finally by one husband – almost! In other words, she'd suffered a lifetime of rejection! All this explains why she was perhaps not the easiest of people to deal with; like all of us she had her own little ways, but her little ways were stranger than most.

A cold wind was blowing, and the air was damp as she sat on Nathaniel Porter's grave, gnawing away at her fingernails, which she always did when deep in thought. The tips of her fingers were stinging from the chill and from the harsh treatment she was meting out to them. It was such a pity that Nathaniel lived on the outer edge of her kingdom for she would have enjoyed having him as a near neighbour.

"I'm going to do it," she said to her dead

friend. "Not today, but sometime in the none too distant future. I just hope that the grand Victorian will not be too displeased. But, maybe, just maybe, he might understand if I explain things to him. I just hope he doesn't show any disapproval and force me to leave. Because where would I go, Nathaniel, where would I go?" In her heart, she knew, of course, exactly where she would go and where she'd feel welcome.

Things came to a head because that very day she had been to the post office and for once there was something waiting for her. She'd always felt that having a post box prevented her from being cut off from the world. Her enormously fat cousin Lorna, for example, would from time to time send her a few pounds to help keep her going, together with news of her latest diet, her latest food binge, and of her even fatter boyfriend. Today there was a missive from a different source – a solicitor's letter informing her that divorce proceedings against her had finally been initiated.

"So, he's done it at last, has he? Well, we'll see about that!" she said to herself. "Perhaps a meeting should be arranged. I'll send him a letter – we could meet somewhere around here – he couldn't really refuse me this one last little request, could he?" Suddenly the wind whistled around the gravestones and made the thickly entwined tendrils of ivy shake.

So, they did meet, husband and wife, but poor Millie had been rejected just once too often for comfort. Unsurprisingly, she did what she knew she would do from first reading the solicitor's letter – the straw that broke the camel's back!

She'd been so right about the Victorian tycoon. To say he was displeased – well, what an understatement! As soon as she had dragged the body into the mausoleum, she had seen strange, flashing lights dotted around as though little fairies were flying through the air holding tiny torches. Never had she seen this manifestation of displeasure before. Added to which, of course, there was the whispering and the little puffs of icy-cold air, the chill of which not even her gas fire could dispel. Then, came the showy pièce de resistance – her cushions were hurled around so fast that their colours became a complete blur. She had expected some resentment, but this was out of all proportion. The smell would not be bad because she had bought extra tins of Airwick. Anyway, there was no other place for the body but here in this mausoleum. It takes up very little room – so convenient and safe now, isn't it?

Inevitably, things soon became so unpleasant that she was forced to leave her home. She had genuinely thought that they all liked her being there, but obviously her presence had merely been tolerated.

How disappointing! Just one more rejection in a long line of rejections!

The snow fell and the cold moon looked down on Millie as she hurried silently among the tombstones. Over one arm she carried a thick blanket and under the other a squashy down-filled pillow. Her capacious coat pockets were filled to overflowing with Mars Bars, and stuffed up the sleeves of her best Fair Isle jumper were a couple of pairs of bed socks. She had been punished, evicted, yet again rejected, but this time she knew where to go. So, with all her might, she pushed the top of Nathaniel's grave to one side and slid into the gap until she was nestling comfortably among his bones, where she would remain until the Mars Bars ran out and death claimed her too.

# The Unfortunate Wife

"It is a dangerous game you are playing, Rowley, my dear. If I give up singing, our whole way of living will be in jeopardy and we shall be forced to live as paupers."

Sir Rowley Sniffkin liked to live as a gentleman; he was, after all, a man possessed of a title, though whether it was genuine or not was open to some debate among his acquaintances. He was enamoured of the life he led, and lavishly entertained the gentry and nobility of Bath; any means of making money was therefore welcome. Nevertheless, he had suddenly decided that someone of his standing, now quickly moving up the social scale, could not possibly have a wife who made a living as an entertainer: too common for words. He was quite right to encourage her to forsake her God-given talent; from thence onward she would sing only for him. The harpsichord would be moved into their bedroom and her sweet voice would thus be heard only in their love nest as she worked even more of her magic on him. She had earned a substantial amount of money singing and the problem now would be to find some other way of keeping their standard of living. Goodness, perhaps he would even have to go out to work – not at all his style! He could, of course, try to write plays, which would not be too demeaning, for it would seem more like a hobby than a serious occupation.

They were living in city with a distinct lack of morals and famous for its overwhelming superficiality among the upper classes. London was the place to be for those at the top of the food chain: a much more discerning and respectable environment. However, if naughtiness and sexual profligacy were one's choice, they were living in the ideal city.

As Lydia and Rowley argued over their financial situation, they heard Clod, their major-domo, clumping down the stairs – why could he never do anything quietly? They kept him on solely (at least, so Rowley thought in his ignorance) because he was cheap to employ and no one else would want him. He did, nevertheless, have his uses – in fact, with his darting eyes and extraordinarily sharp hearing he made an excellent spy. If Sir Rowley and Lydia ever wanted to know any of the malicious gossip and scandalous intrigue that abounded among their acquaintances, he was the fount of all knowledge to whom they always referred.

The matrimonial couple, as well as arguing, were also preparing for the rather grand gathering that they were hosting that evening. Palgrave, Lydia's maid was already in the opulent bedchamber preparing her mistress's gown and makeup. Lydia had decided that she would try and look even more spectacular for the occasion than usual – in view of their special guest. Her wildly expensive wig had been arranged lovingly by Palgrave on its stand with not a curl out of place. Even lower than usual, she was sure her décolletage would draw the eyes of every man in the room – indeed the hostess with the mostest!

She sat in front of the mirror as Palgrave anointed her still pretty face with a toxic, white mixture of lead, mercury and arsenic that would eventually completely ruin her skin. To hide her pox marks, the worst of which was luckily at the corner of her rose-bud mouth, a velvet, diamond-shaped beauty patch was glued in place which signified a willingness to flirt; already her tongue could be seen provocatively licking the inside of her mouth. Her makeup was completed by red dye for her lips and brownish rouge for her cheeks.

Needless to say, her gown was a dream of a

creation: bows, puffs, ribbons and lace, all in the most vibrant of colours. However, such was the fashion that Browne, Sir Rowley's personal servant, was doing pretty much the same to his master's face. Rowley's high heels and hose, together with the brilliant, shiny material and colours, made him look rather like a peacock, which was the whole idea – distinctly foppish! Really a cross-dresser!

"I do so hope that Lady Scrunch will be as awful as usual." This was Rowley speaking of their guest of honour, the she-dragon, the arch-gossip of society who had travelled from London, not just to attend their gathering, but also for other social events. If the evening were a success, the names of Sir Rowley and Lady Sniffkin might even reach the ears of some minor royal personage in the drawing rooms of London, which would do their reputation no harm at all – or so they hoped.

Lydia winked an eye at Sir Rowley and gave him the best view she could of her ample breasts, just as a little practice for what was to come, careful, however, not to over-excite him, for she didn't want her beauty preparations spoiled: it had taken Palgrave such a long time to achieve this picture of perfection. Although, indeed, there were some men who liked women to look slightly dishevelled – it made their imagination run on wheels. "Well," she said, "we all know how the old dear simply adores the most licentious and shocking tales possible. We shall have to keep Clod on his toes so that he misses nothing. And then you, husband dear, can whisper all those wonderfully cruel, witty tit-bits into Lady Scrunch's ever-hungry ear. She feeds on nastiness and other people's misfortunes . . . well, don't we all!" she added with a wicked laugh.

The clip-clopping of horses' hooves and the chatter of well-bred voices, although not all totally genuine, could be heard approaching the house along the fine Palladian crescent. Soon the Sniffkin drawing room was filled by the hunting set, by the poseurs of the area, by aspiring musicians and artists, by failed actors and writers and even by bona fide members of the nobility.

As usual Lady Scrunch arrived late in the proceedings: in other words, a grand entrance in front of a captive audience. She was accompanied by two black-skinned, golden-turbaned servants. As she moved proudly upright through the room, the gentlemen bowed respectfully and the ladies gave a slight curtsey of acknowledgement – she loved this. In London she was just one more spiteful- tongued, high-born woman among many, while here she was really someone special. The usual gossiping had started long before her arrival as had the drinking – mostly sparkling wine. Palgrave had been giving her mistress wine during her evening preparations to steady her nerves and thus Lydia was probably well advanced in her consumption long before the arrival of her first guest: not a very wise move as it turned out.

Lady Scrunch was no vision of beauty – her teeth had long ago given up the ghost, victim to the poisonous whitener with which she had treated them – even gunpowder was one of its ingredients To possess white, sparkling teeth was a predominant obsession with most women. Lady Scrunch having lost them all, decided to have hers replaced with some made of wood which made her face sink inward. As was the fashion, she plumped her cheeks out with pieces of cork, so teeth in general, not surprisingly, refused to fit well and the result was a lisp, which very soon became all the rage in fashionable society.

Soon, Lydia was somewhat the worse for wear and innocently made a very bitchy remark to her honoured guest, concerning a mutual acquaintance … "What a strange little person she is – perhaps some sort of problem common in her family: brain deficiency, or the beginning of madness, something of that nature, I suspect. It would certainly worry me if she were of my blood and I would question my own sanity."

Unfortunately, this strange, little person was Lady Scrunch's niece of whom she was rather fond.

Straightaway, her face appropriately scrunched up in displeasure and the knives were well and truly out. An almighty argument ensued; poor Rowley tried in vain to interfere, but he knew that his ultimate dream of one day being invited to court was disappearing by the second. He and Lydia would become social outcasts. Then Lydia completely lost control, grabbed hold of her opponent's wig and flung it over the balcony so that it landed on a damp flower bed. Thus, Lady Scrunch's bald head, shining in the candlelight, was there for the entire world to see. The cork from her poor cheeks had not survived the fracas either and lay in a little pile on the beautiful carpet: as, indeed, did her wooden teeth.

Worse was to follow, however, at which point Rowley and Lydia wanted the earth to swallow them, oceans to rise up to drown them or perhaps, better still, the whole city to ignite in a ball of fire and disappear into nothingness.

Staggering in from the general direction of the servants' quarters, it was now Clod's turn to make a grand entrance. In each hand he was holding a half-empty bottle of sparkling wine, slurping and guzzling gustily from each one in turn. His legs were bent at the knees like a ninety-year-old and he was rip-roaringly drunk: drunk as a lord, you might say, which fitted rather aptly with Rowley and Lydia's aspirations that were now rather obviously never to be realised. He tottered up to Lydia, put his arms around her and gave her a loud, soggy kiss on the forehead. "My baby, my little daughter, my little darling!" he slurred.

The great secret had finally been revealed and, once said, could never be unsaid. The tension could have been cut with a knife, so full of wonderment and disbelief was the room. Rowley, totally unaware, had completely lost consciousness and lay face down on the carpet. The guests were so happy to have seen this drama, for it would be spoken of for years, but the happiest person there was poor, bald, toothless Lady Scrunch. She would never have to plot her revenge or to lie awake in the darkness of the night planning Lydia's come-uppance, for the major-domo had done her work for her. Forever after she would smirk remembering the evening when Lady Rowley Sniffkin had suddenly reverted to plain Lydia Clod.

# When He Sleeps

They always say that your dreams come back to haunt you and that, therefore, you can never escape the things you have done.

He says that this is not true, but he is wrong because I listen to his slumbers and I know that every nasty, terrifying dream he dreams is his just desert. I hope he spends the rest of eternity dreaming them!

He lies here at my side, mumbling and moaning in his sleep and I hope there is a lot of pain there! He lies here at my side, sweating and smelling like the dirty pig he is. However, I take that back because it is in the nature of pigs to be as they are, but he is supposed to be one of God's children; yet another living proof that the divine design is fallible and flawed!

I think, from his mutterings that his hell tonight is of the extra-terrestrial kind; I so enjoy these dreams amid the stars, because they are truly horrible. As his dream becomes more vivid and more distressing, the whole event will be narrated to me, because, even in sleep, he can never keep his big mouth shut. I will be able to witness his suffering close at hand and gauge its severity!

Yes, there he goes; crawling, creeping along, fingernails broken and bloody, thinking that it's impossible to keep going like this for much longer. I know this dream and I know he will keep dragging himself along in this alien place; a world where every breath sears his lungs and every pore is filled with a curious sand-like substance. All he sees are bare rocks and, behind them, the cold, shadowy light from a dimming sunset, the like of which he has seen nowhere else except on this inhospitable planet. I almost know this terrible place better than he does! His ears and mine too, are filled with the sound of his rasping attempts to breathe in the planet's dense atmosphere. He is conscious also of a strange, plaintive, childish voice that vibrates clearly, even in the stifling, heavy air. Why this should be, so he has no idea – it really is far beyond his imagination!

Now, he is beginning his customary ranting against God for placing him in this extra-terrestrial hell. It never registers with him, of course, that hell is precisely what he deserves; for he is a man without conscience, without remorse.

Aren't you, my dear?

Somewhere, in the recesses of his mind is born the idea that this is not reality. Has God, perhaps, conjured up for him only, this nightmarish illusion, this dreadful dream? Why is he unable to wake up, to escape the torment he is suffering?   Oh, but it is going to get worse for you … my dear; much, much worse!

In the distance, through the gloom, he can see a small figure; but is it really there? If he closes his eyes or turns his head away, does the figure truly still exist, or will it only return when he again opens his eyes or turns his head towards it? What is reality and what is illusion in this strange world?  Little does he know that the tiny image is going to be there for the duration of the dream (for the rest of eternity, in fact!); by now, he must know that and have got used to the sight. Amazingly, he still doesn't know what it signifies!

Suddenly, he espies a strange, winding, silver stream that glows in the alien twilight, and curls its way sinuously, snake-like, between the rocks. As the hideous sunset wanes and complete darkness takes over, still this silvery serpent gleams and throbs and pulsates! Thirst is now his prime sensation, even more acute than the pain in his hands and feet. I can see him licking his lips, his repulsive, little, pink tongue darting in and out, in and out of the dark cavern. Does the glowing stream contain something that could possibly assuage his thirst? Any liquid would do; however bitter, however rank. I know the answer to that, but he doesn't! Not yet!

With the utmost discomfort he drags himself across the black landscape: his hands tugging and tearing at the eiderdown. His body, beside me, jerks as he feels the sharp, gravelly earth piercing his skin through tattered clothes. Suddenly, above him, the vast darkness is rent by a fiery thunderbolt and through the bedroom curtains, as though on cue, come flashes of forked lightning; but it is only here, in rural Hertfordshire, that they are followed by thirst-quenching rain.

On his alien planet, all remains parched and his mouth most parched of all. The thunder and lightning continue, illuminating his way, as he continues his painful progress towards the stream. A strong, unpleasant, metallic smell emanates from it. As he finally manages to place his hand in the silvery mass, all he can feel is a disgusting slime that fails to give relief to the pulsing pain of his torn hands, let alone to his thirst!

Suddenly the earth trembles, as it always does at this point in the dream, so he should be used to it by now; the horror of what he is about to see, tempered by familiarity... but, no, it fails completely, to register in his memory. Once again, I watch his unseeing eyes staring, full of dread, at the sight he sees in his dream-world. His mouth gapes open, fish-like, as he tries in vain to give voice to his terror. The monster cometh... my dear!

Look at it ...there, in all its ugliness! Not the usual, alien monster of Science Fiction, but a true monster; huge and black and evil with massive wings that sizzle and singe, letting out the pungent smell of sulphur! The Devil himself, no less – what he truly deserves! The little figure at the back of the dream stands there watching over what is taking place, never participating in the action. It is at this point, the dream usually ends, so fearful is the revolting vision of the appalling, winged apparition,

It appears tonight that the protagonist is going to be someone else; not the Devil, not this spirit of darkness who has suddenly evaporated into nothingness, but someone good and kind and, above all, innocent; my son, my darling son, my lovely boy, destined to die because of his accursed father's negligence and arrogance; the snorting animal who snuffles and grunts beside me.

"David!" he rasps out as our little son approaches him. Since his death two years ago, never have I seen my son in my dreams and I truly envy what the wheezing wretch is experiencing. It has taken two whole years for him to recognise the diminutive figure of his own son who has waited so patiently in the background of his dreams!

"David!" he calls out again and watches as the little boy, holding out his arms to feel his father's love around him, runs towards him. The gravelly earth is slippery and he loses his balance, sliding inexorably towards the silvery slime. In he tumbles, and his childish voice, which carries like a song in the suffocating air, cries out for help. "Daddy, daddy, help me! Please help me!"

His father's only reply is the same as it was two years ago. "Don't be silly, David, you're a big boy now! You know how to swim!"

The brutish man lets his only child slip away into the slime, as he let him disappear under the waters of the river that flows near our house. Two years ago, neglectful, uncaring, he sat in the long grass, amid the scarlet poppies, scribbling away at what was to become his first best-seller as our precious son died. This time too preoccupied with his own pain and discomfort, he lets him perish in the ooze of the silvery stream!

The dream continues; obviously not a traumatic enough event to awaken the slumbering pig from his nightmare! No lesson learnt there! No redemption and no absolution!

All at once, a terrible rumbling fills the air of this otherworld and there comes, rolling along the ground, a huge boulder as though pushed by some galactic giant. It comes faster and faster, making a noise greater than any thunderclap, or earthquake. Finally, it reaches its victim and he screams out in agony…

So, something has finally awakened you from your long sleep, has it… my dear? It certainly doesn't seem to have done you much good, for you don't look at all hunky-dory! Your face has turned a most unattractive shade of blue… I could show it to you it in my hand-mirror if you like… Are you having trouble with your breathing? Not choking, are you? A squeezing pain in your chest…! You know, I think you are having another of your little heart attacks! It must have been an awful dream you've just had!

What did you just say? Help? Help…! Help from me? I don't think so! However, on second thoughts, why not? I'll do the decent thing…my dear! I will put an end to your suffering… You see this nice, frilly, Ariel-white pillow you have been resting that nasty little head of yours on? It's the ideal tool for death by suffocation, don't you think? At any minute now, it's going to send you into a permanent dream world. I devoutly hope and pray that it's a world full of nightmares of the most devilish kind.

This is the punishment that I, your judge, am meting out to you; for the wages of sin is death. Before you go on your journey, I think I should perhaps remind you, if it's of any interest to you, that today would have been David's seventh birthday. He was only a baby, five years old, when you so cruelly and arrogantly left him to his own devices.

So, a long goodnight, and may the undiscovered country from whose bourn no traveller returns be a damned unpleasant one…my dear!

# Who Said That?

The ghost stood outside the church. He was feeling somewhat out of sorts because it was such a beautiful day that he would, in normal circumstances, have liked to indulge in a spot of sunbathing. However, of course, since his demise, that wasn't possible, was it? So he was decidedly down in the dumps, which meant that his aura, usually strong and vibrant, was tending to wax and wane; sometimes you could almost see him (and sometimes almost not).

Thankfully, today he was mostly invisible. After all it would not be at all appropriate to have a ghost in full view during a wedding ceremony, would it? As cigarettes seemed to have gone out of fashion it was unlikely that he could pass himself off as a puff of smoke – or even as a whiff of burning incense because it wasn't that sort of church.

It was a small wedding. There was Bill the butcher and his missis, Fred from the hardware shop with his plumpy-lumpy daughter Miriam,

Old Mrs Ragwort who 'did' up at the manor and so on and so forth. All togged up in their Sunday best!

The ghost was at that moment drifting aimlessly at the side of Miss Dunwiddy, secretary to Jones and Jenkins, solicitors, when suddenly the bells began to ring and the organ to thunder. This, together with the screaming of toddlers, playing hide and seek among the gravestones, caused the ghost, who didn't realise that he could be heard, to exclaim, "Blimey! What a bloody noise!"

To which Miss Dunwiddy, looking anxiously around, retorted, "Who said that?"

"I did"

"Why?"

"Because I felt like it!"

"Not a very pleasant thing to say, was it?"

"No, but then I'm not a very pleasant person, am I?"

Which probably went a long way to explain why he was still earth bound, still hovering around the village, when really, he should have been in the great beyond enjoying his just deserts!

With the guests in their allotted places, the bridegroom waiting anxiously at the altar, and the ghost wandering unseen, up and down the aisle, the bride finally arrived holding tightly onto her father who must, at a quick estimate, have anointed himself with at least a pint of aftershave. The organist at this point revved up to maximum volume, as the cringe-making star choir boy, Stewart Swarbrick, started churning out, "Oh, for the Wings of a Dove".

Casting a quick spectral eye over the congregation the ghost observed that the only notable absentee from the happy event was the bride's prospective mother-in-law who, it appeared, was suffering from one of her sick headaches and would be spending the day, supine, in her darkened bedroom.

The music, thankfully for the moment over, the vicar stepped forward to play his crucial role in the proceedings and was just about to address the gathering with the familiar opening words to the service, when the ghost, who by now was sitting on the altar steps, realised that there was someone standing at the open church door. There was collective gasp from the congregation and as he floated up to the ceiling, he was able to see that, far from being confined to her bed, the bridegroom's mother had arrived to play her part in the drama.

There she was, a vision in black mourning garb, standing silhouetted against the sun that streamed into the church, her legs apart, aiming a rifle at the bride; an SG 550 assault rifle with its side-folding skeletonised buttstock and with a test range of 300 metres – if the ghost wasn't mistaken. In other words, certain curtains for the bride if she didn't do a nifty side-step.

"You little floozy! No way are you going to marry our Bert. I'll see you buried first, see if I don't!"

The ghost, however, feeling an uncharacteristic swell of charity, was by now thinking to himself that it would be a bit of a shame if the young couple weren't able to tie the knot and so floated down from his vantage point into the aisle. He then strode purposefully towards the enemy and bravely looked directly down the barrel of the rifle, completely forgetting that, as he was already dead, a bullet was not actually going to make much difference to him! His aura was now plainly visible to all, which caused several people in the congregation to keel over in terror!

"Lay down your arms this instant", his disembodied voice commanded. "No good will come of such a rash gesture!"

"Who said that, who said that?" everyone was asking as his words echoed up towards the vaulted ceiling, up towards the top of the tall stained glass windows, up the pillars whose carved cherubs were looking down upon the drama, until they eventually dropped down again to reach the ears of Bert's mother who instantly handed over the rifle and, open-mouthed, watched it move, as though of its own accord, back towards the altar. Which all went to prove that the word is mightier than the rifle!

The vicar by this time had virtually given up the will to live and was having a quick slurp of the brandy that he always kept under the altar for strictly medicinal purposes! As for the bridesmaids – well, they were lying in a frothy, pink heap in front of the lectern indulging themselves in a histrionic show of hysteria.

However, eventually, after Bert's mum had been carted off in a police car, the wedding took place and, as far as we know, the newlyweds lived happily ever after!

The ghost – what of him? Well, he was feeling very odd, something very strange was happening, for he had the distinct sensation that the church and all the people therein were moving away from him and that he was standing alone in a state of absolute nothingness; a void, a complete emptiness. Not darkness, just greyness. Then suddenly he saw something in the distance and felt himself being propelled towards it. It was a tunnel, and in he went... At the end of it he could see a light towards which he was being irresistibly drawn. The ghost very much liked what he saw there and thought that he perhaps might like to stay there permanently – which just goes to show you what a smidgen of charity will do in the right circumstances!

# Also by
# Vonnie Giles
www.uppbooks.com

Lightning Source UK Ltd.
Milton Keynes UK
UKHW021141021020
370914UK00009B/211